PUT ON YOUR MASK OR JUST BE YOURSELF

MARIA DE VIDA

Prime Seven Media
518 Landmann St.
Tomah City, WI 54660

Printed in the United States of America

Table of Contents

Introduction

Put on Your Mask or Just Be Yourself is a profound exploration of the human struggle between authenticity and the pressures of the world around us. It's a story that asks us to question the masks we wear—and the reasons we choose to hide our true selves. In a world full of expectations and assumptions, this book invites you to take a deeper look at what it means to truly be free: to let go of the need to fit in, and embrace who we really are, without fear or compromise.

At the heart of the story are Maria and John, two people who are more alike than they initially realize.

Maria is someone who has always believed in the goodness of people and the possibility for the world to be better. She believes that everyone has the potential to become the best version of themselves. Her heart is full of hope, and she strives to give to others—to uplift them in any way she can. Due to her mysterious past, she faces a world that constantly tests her, pushes her to the edge, and even tries to kill her. Yet through every trial, Maria never loses hope. She clings to the belief that things can improve, and that people can rise above their circumstances.

John, a Miami Police Department cop and a strong-headed, by-the-book kind of guy, is a true leader in his space. Growing up in Brazil, he has a real zest for life and has seen both the bright and dark sides of humanity. He's followed the rules for most of his life—but after meeting Maria, something begins to shift. His interest in stepping outside the lines starts to grow.

Unbeknownst to them, Maria and John share a deeper connection through John's uncle, Lee—a former inspector whose mysterious death raises unsettling questions about its true cause and the greater powers at play. As they grow closer, the unbelievable discoveries they uncover will require both of them to face the truth. They come to understand that material things don't matter—they're temporary. What truly matters is the kind of heart you carry, and how you choose to grow it.

This story takes you around the world—from the friendly yet dark urban streets of Manchester to the chaotic energy of Rio de Janeiro. It's never short on action, uncovering both the shadow and the light in humanity. Packed with adventure, mystery, and drama, this book will take you through a range of emotions that might just make you ask yourself: **"Why am I trying to be 'THE BEST' for everyone else, when I'm not even being 'THE BEST' for myself?"**

When their worlds collide, Maria and John are forced to confront the parts of themselves they've long tried to hide. In doing so, they discover that the journey to true freedom isn't about fighting the world—but about embracing who we are, even when it feels impossible. Their paths toward self-discovery will lead you through moments of heartbreak, tension, and unexpected revelations. This is a story of emotional growth, of love and trust, and of the strength that comes from being unapologetically yourself—even when the world doesn't make it easy.

This book will make you reflect on the roles we all play, the masks we wear, and the deep desire for connection that lives in every one of us. It's a reminder that the most important thing we can do is find the courage to be who we truly are. And in doing so, we may discover a kind of peace and strength we never thought possible.

It will also make you question…

What if life is not what it seems?
What if we're not meant to stay the same—but to grow in ways we don't yet understand?
We aren't born with the answers… but do we have the power to find them?

Why does the human eye always search for more?
Why do we always crave something beyond what we already have?
Could it be… that the more we possess, the emptier we feel?

What if, in all this seeking, we've lost sight of who we truly are?
Have we forgotten ourselves somewhere along the way?
Have we tucked the child within us deep inside… locked it away, just to fit in, to be liked, to meet others' expectations?

What would happen if we stopped defining ourselves by what the world tells us we should be—and started asking:
Who am I, really?

Can I ever truly know what I want…
Or am I just chasing the shadows of desires I have been taught
to have?

It's so much easier to judge… to envy… to criticize.
But what if the real answers are found in supporting each other,
in truly appreciating what we already have?

After all, isn't it true?
No one is perfect.
Not even the person you see in the mirror.

Chapter 1

1994. Somewhere in Manchester.

It was early morning, the sun was just rising, and the streets were being bathed in its golden rays. Everything felt still, the peace broken only by the occasional passing car.

Maria had just returned to her apartment after her usual morning run. She was in her late twenties, with long, wavy, light-brown hair that fell effortlessly over her shoulders. Her deep brown eyes gleamed in the sunlight, giving her an enchanting look that was hard to ignore.

Stepping into her cozy apartment, Maria heard the soft buzz of her alarm clock echoing from the living room. She walked over and turned it off—a retro clock from the 1950s, perfectly matching the vintage charm of her space. The apartment was filled with lush green plants, creating a serene, almost tropical oasis. This was her sanctuary—her personal paradise.

"Right, time to get ready for the day," Maria said to herself with a smile.

She turned on the TV, and the familiar guitar riff of Lenny Kravitz's "Are You Gonna Go My Way" filled the room. She cranked up the volume and danced her way toward the bathroom, dropping her clothes on the way. The beat energized her as she showered, preparing for what promised to be a big day.

Freshly showered and wrapped in a soft white robe, she heard a knock at the door. Curious, she peeked through the peephole. It was Mrs. Evans—a sharply dressed elderly woman with a small dog tucked under her arm, wearing her usual expression of disapproval.

Maria turned off the TV, smiled mischievously, and opened the door.

"Well, well! What is going on here…?" Mrs. Evans exclaimed, eyeing Maria from head to toe. "Opening the door in such a state—and that music! What is this place—a nightclub?"

Maria chuckled. "What's the matter, Mrs. Evans? Don't like my look?" she teased, her voice light but confident.

With a playful smirk, she let her robe slip from her shoulders, revealing black underwear and the intricate tattoo that spanned her entire back—a vivid, sprawling design. A large rose sat at the center; its petals wrapped in the coils of a fierce dragon. The delicate leaves and blossoms extended down her left arm like a living vine.

"And what do you think of my tattoo?" Maria asked with a twinkle in her eye.

"Too much for you, perhaps?"

Mrs. Evans gasped, clearly shaken. "Good heavens! Tattoos everywhere… What a disgraceful sight! You young people these days—always trying to shock with your… drawings."

Maria crossed her arms, calm and unbothered. "Funny how people are quick to judge what they see on the outside without ever taking a moment to understand what's inside," she said softly. "It's like judging a book by its cover, isn't it, Mrs. Evans?"

"Ah… what a disgrace!" Mrs. Evans snapped, her voice trembling with indignation. "When will you finally learn to behave with some decency and respect?"

Her eyes shifted to the side. A little boy—about seven or eight— was peeking from his doorway, curiously watching the exchange.

"And you, Mikey! What are you staring at, you nosy little boy? Go tell your mother to pay the rent! I'm not here to wait on you forever!" Mrs.Evans said.

Maria quickly pulled her robe back around her and leaned slightly out of her doorway to see. But before she could say anything, Mikey darted back inside his apartment, startled and afraid.

Annoyed by what she'd just heard, Maria turned back to Mrs. Evans. Her voice stayed calm, but her eyes held a quiet fire.

"Mrs. Evans… when you start treating others with a little kindness, then—and only then—will I consider changing my behavior. Neither I nor anyone else here has done anything to offend you. Yet you're constantly dissatisfied."

She took a deep breath before continuing. Mrs. Evans stood stiffly, arms crossed, glaring in disbelief.

"You know what?" Maria said with a faint smile. She folded her towel neatly and placed it on the chair beside her, then picked up her clothes and began dressing. "I think it's time you started appreciating human relationships. It's not too late."

"Ha! Me? Appreciate human relationships?" Mrs. Evans scoffed. "And you think you're the one to teach me manners? You, who has no manners at all? You, who—"

Maria raised a hand gently, cutting her off.

"Enough, Mrs. Evans. Look at yourself. You've been insulting me non-stop, and yet I haven't said a single harsh word back—out of respect. But don't mistake my kindness for weakness. There's a line, and you're dangerously close to crossing it. You don't own anyone. We're all human beings—equal in every way. So please… have a good day."

With that, Maria closed the door—firmly, but without a slam. Mrs. Evans stood frozen for a moment, stunned. Then, with a mumble under her breath, she turned and walked away.

After some time, in the next room, Ellie, Mikey's mother, moved quietly around the kitchen, making breakfast. Her movements were slow, deliberate, but Mikey noticed the subtle change in her—the way her eyes, usually warm and comforting, seemed distant, like she was somewhere far away. Ellie tried to hide it, but the amount of her worry was clear, and Mikey, with his keen awareness, saw it immediately.

He signed to her gently, "What's wrong, Mum?"

Ellie hesitated, forcing a soft smile, but it didn't reach her eyes. She signed back quickly, "Everything is fine, Mikey. Don't worry." Her hands were trembling as she handed him the bowl of milk and cereal. She could not hide the anxiety building inside her. Where would she find the money to pay her rent… She needed a moment alone, so she told Mikey she was going to the bathroom and left the room in haste.

Behind the closed door, Ellie turned on the faucet, letting the sound of water running mask her quiet sobs. She wiped her eyes quickly, but the tears would not stop. She could not keep pretending everything was fine.

A quick knock at the door startled Mikey, and he rushed to open it. There, standing in the doorway, was Maria. Mikey's face lit up with joy, his heart easing as they embraced. Her presence was a comfort, like a light in the darkness.

Maria, just like Mikey, used sign language to communicate, and without skipping a beat, she began the conversation.

"How are you, Mikey?" Maria signed with a soft smile, her fingers moving fluidly, showing genuine care.

"I'm okay, and you?" Mikey signed back, but his eyes kept drifting toward the bathroom, where he knew his mother was struggling.

"I'm fine, but Mikey…" Maria's hands paused midair, a thoughtful look crossing her face. "I saw you earlier, listening by the door. That is not something you should do."

Mikey's face tightened with guilt. "I know… I was just looking. And she… she's so cruel, like an old witch. I'm afraid of her," he signed, trying to explain.

Maria's face softened, her eyes full of understanding. She gently knelt before him, placing her hands on his shoulders, looking into his eyes with tenderness. The words that followed came slowly and lovingly.

"Mikey," she signed, "there are no bad people, you know that?" She paused, letting the silence hang for a moment. "Some people… they have lost something precious. They have lost hope, right here." She pointed her finger to his chest, right above his heart. "When they lose hope in themselves, they hurt others because they're hurting too."

Mikey's gaze followed her hand, resting on the place she pointed to. His eyes filled with confusion, but Maria's voice, her touch, made the world around them calm just enough for him to understand. She continued, her fingers moving with certainty.

"Before you judge someone, Mikey, you must first understand them. You must walk in their shoes. Everyone has their own story, and there is always more than one side."

Maria stood back up, her hand resting nicely on Mikey's shoulder as he absorbed her words. The moment between them felt heavy, but it was filled with compassion and truth—one that Mikey would carry with him long after the conversation ended.

At that moment, Ellie stood aside, moved by Maria's words. Life had not been easy for her—raising her deaf son on her own. But Maria had always been there for them, offering help in any way she could.

"Maria, that's so kind of you," Ellie said, walking toward them. "You always—"

But Maria interrupted her before she could say more. "Ellie…" she said, then turned to Mikey, signaling for him to finish his breakfast. Maria pulled Ellie aside, her expression serious as she tried to understand what was really happening with them.

Meanwhile, in the neighbouring apartment, Mrs. Evans was making tea, humming softly to herself. Every so often, she peeked out her window to see what was going on outside.

Suddenly, there was a knock at her door. Mrs. Evans went to open it, and when she did, she was surprised to see Maria standing there, smiling warmly.

"Hello, Mrs. Evans!" Maria greeted her cheerfully.

"YOU?" Mrs. Evans asked, her eyes widening in confusion.

"Yes, that's right" Maria replied with a smile. "I might be too much for you today, but I've got some good news."

"Really?" Mrs. Evans raised an eyebrow, her arms crossed as she waited for Maria to elaborate, her tone dripping with sarcasm.

"Of course!" Maria said, pulling out her wallet from her sports bag. "Here, Mrs. Evans. This is for Ellie and Mikey—for last month and this month."

She handed Mrs. Evans the money with a calm, steady hand. Maria's kindness was a powerful force, Mrs. Evans looked at the money, unsure of how to react.

Before Mrs. Evans could fully process what was happening, Maria added with a smile, "Oh! I almost forgot! Here, this is also for Ellie's rent for the coming month, since she will not be staying in your apartment anymore."

Maria's eyes were steady, unwavering, as she quietly awaited a response.

"But how is that possible?" Mrs. Evans asked, confusion and disbelief in her voice.

Maria smiled warmly, as if it were all perfectly simple. "Oh, don't worry. They will still be your neighbours," she added.

"Neighbours? But how? I own most of the apartments here," Mrs. Evans replied, still skeptical.

"Yes, you're absolutely right," Maria said, nodding. "Except for mine. I own it myself. Ellie and Mikey will be living with me. Look, see," she added, pointing outside the door.

Mrs. Evans craned her neck to get a better view and saw Ellie and Mikey standing at the entrance of Maria's apartment. Mikey, upon noticing the old woman, immediately began pulling faces and sticking out his tongue at her.

Maria's eyes narrowed, and without missing a beat, she gave Mikey a sharp look. Ellie quickly ushered him inside, guiding him away from the door.

"What do you think you're doing, Maria?" Mrs. Evans asked, her tone now cold.

"Me?" Maria replied, feigning innocence. "Nothing. In fact, I would even suggest we have tea one day, just to show you that I have no bad intentions and that the world is not such a terrible place after all," she said with a calm smile.

"Oh yes, of course……... I would not even drink water with people like you" …… Mrs. Evans snapped before slamming the door in Maria's face.

Maria stood there for a moment, the door now closed between them, her smile fading into a sigh. "Well, at least I tried" she muttered to herself.

Glancing at her watch, she suddenly realised the time. "Oh no, I'm late!" …. she exclaimed, turning on her heel and rushing toward the exit.

As she ran down the street, she saw the bus pulling away in the distance. Her frustration bubbled up, but she could not help but laugh lightheartedly. "No…. no…...no…... Really?" …. she said, raising her head to the sky, as if asking for answers from above. "Of course, it's me. Who else but me?" ….. she muttered, her smile returning as she shook her head, resigned to her fate.

Anyway, Maria began scanning the street, hoping to find another way to get there. She could not afford to be late, not today of all days—the grand opening of another free restaurant for homeless people. It was an event that always filled her with a deep sense of purpose.

And there she was, just a little behind schedule. As she reached the restaurant, she was met by a long line of people standing with eyes full of hope and gratitude, each one silently thankful for the meal they were about to receive. At the entrance, stood Martin, a close friend of Maria's. The moment he spotted her, he could not help but tease her, his voice full of a familiar, warmth. "Maria, finally! Where the hell have you been?"

Maria chuckled, her heart light. "Oh, come on, calm down! I was watching a TV show—an amazing series, by the way. It's going to be a hit," she replied, waving her hand dismissively.

Martin raised an eyebrow, half-amused and half-frustrated. "Seriously, Maria? Seriously?" he said, shaking his head.

Maria just laughed, brushing it off as she made her way closer to the entrance. Despite the hustle of the moment, there was something comforting in their exchange. The energy around them was a mix of anticipation and compassion.

To calm Martin down, Maria quickly responded, "Of course, I'm not. Today is a big day for me too. I just missed the bus. So don't worry, just go inside, and let's get started."

Martin, still a bit skeptical, smirked. "Of course, Maria, if it's not the bus, it's something else. You never have a normal day. Everything around you is always a mess." He muttered, walking inside, shaking his head.

The day continued, filled with a lot of joy. The crowd of people began to flow in, and a group of volunteers, some of whom were homeless themselves, started serving warm food. Amidst the movement and activity, Maria's eyes searched the crowd for one person in particular.

"Where's Jessica?" Maria asked, her voice tinged with concern.

"I don't know," Martin responded, his face lighting up with a hint of jest. "She's running late just like you. She should have been here by now."

However, Maria couldn't shake the feeling of unease. She continued serving food, her mind distracted, unable to ignore the worry gnawing at her. After a while, she couldn't take it anymore.

"I'm going to look for her" Maria said.

"Alright, go ahead," Martin replied. "There are enough people here to help, but hurry, before she gets into any trouble."

"I hope she's okay" Maria murmured. "She's been clean for a while now. She has not taken anything…"

She paused, then added, "But I know where to find her."

At that moment, Jessica was in a strip club, her eyes darting nervously. She was not supposed to be there. She was looking for something—something to numb the bitter emptiness inside— but instead, she found herself back in the place she had once worked, a place that had haunted her, a place that could pull her back under like a tidal wave.

She tried to leave, quietly, hoping no one would notice, but it was already too late. One of the bouncers grabbed her roughly by the arm, his grip firm and unyielding, dragging her in one of the booths next to the bar, where the club boss was having a private meeting.

"What's this about, Benny?" ….. Franco, the business partner, asked with a cold and calculating gaze as he observed the situation. "Who is she? Did she overhear our conversation?"

Benny's eyes flickered over to Jessica, who was visibly shaking, trying to hold herself together. She was trapped, and she knew it. "She's an old worker of mine" …… Benny muttered…… "She used to work here, but I have not seen her in a while…… What are you doing here?" ….. He asked her.

"Nothing!" Jessica stammered…… "I swear, nothing! I just—I didn't mean—"

Before Benny could respond, a figure stepped into the club, tall and commanding. It was Maria. The tension in the room thickened in an instant. She held the security guard in front of her, with a gun pointed at his head as she walked in.

"Well, well," …. Maria said…… "Looks like we've got quite the party going on here." ….. Her eyes scanned the room, searching for Jessica.

Franco's hand went instinctively to his own weapon, but Benny, seeing the situation unfold, gestured for him to hold off. He knew Maria. They had crossed paths before, and he knew she was not someone you played games with.

Maria walked towards Jessica, her eyes never leaving the girl's trembling form. She pushed Benny aside with effortless strength, her stare hardening. Franco gestured with his eyes to the bouncers to grab her. They moved towards her guns raised. Without a word, she shot three of the bouncers in rapid succession—one in the leg, one in the shoulder, and the last in the opposite leg. They crumpled to the ground, groaning, unable to move.

Jessica's heart raced, her breath coming in shallow gasps. She didn't know whether to feel relief or fear. Maria had stepped into her life with the force of a hurricane.

Maria pointed the gun at the bouncer who was holding Jessica.…
"Let her go." … She didn't need to raise her voice; her presence
was enough.

The bouncer glanced at his boss Benny, and with his permission
he let the girl go. Jessica could barely believe what was happening.
The bouncers hesitated for a split second, then, seeing no choice,
backed away. Maria didn't lower the gun. She simply waited,
watching them, until they retreated to the sides.

Slowly, Jessica stood up, her knees weak. She walked over to Maria,
unsure of what to say, unsure of what any of this meant. Her hand
reached for the counter, but Maria stopped her, pulling her up.

"You're not alone anymore," Maria said, guiding Jessica to
the bar, sitting her down beside her. Maria's touch was warm,
comforting.…

"I'm sorry, I'm really sorry. I know I promised" Jessica whispered,
still in disbelief.

Maria's eyes softened. "You know sometimes it's OK to not
be OK, you do not deserve to be here. You don't deserve to be
anyone's pawn." She let out a long breath, as if releasing pressure
that had been there far too long. "No one should ever be afraid of
the world, Jessica, and I'm not going to let you be afraid anymore."

For the first time in a long while, Jessica felt something inside
her—something that had been buried beneath the pain and fear.
It was hope, fragile but real.

Maria sat there, her attention unwavering. "So, Benny, what is
going on? Who is your friend?"

Beni stiffened, shifting uncomfortably, his words stumbling over each other, but before he could gather himself, Franco interjected.

"And who are you?" Franco asked, his eyes sharp, assessing. He slid into the seat next to her, motioning for a drink with an easy confidence that did not match the tone of the situation.

Maria met his gaze, her eyes locking with his. "Me?" she said with a smirk. "Lucky for you, I'm not a cop, but I know plenty who are."

She turned her attention back to Benny…… "Right, Benny? How is your son, by the way? Still in prison? Is he doing well?"

Benny's face tightened, a flicker of discomfort crossing his features. "Maria, just take the girl and go," he muttered… "I don't even know why she is here. But I bet you do. I can always put her back on the pole if you want, right, Jessica?" His words were right on target, so precisely directed. "I know that is what you want. But you know what, Maria? Sometimes, no matter how much you help some people, it's just not enough. They don't even want to help themselves."

Maria stood powerless, she knew he was right. She could not say NO to the truth it was not in her nature. Her eyes drilled into him, and with a look she told the bartender to pour her a drink, letting his words sink in. Then, without missing a beat, she set her glass down. "You're right," she said quietly, almost as if she was reflecting on something deeper. "You're absolutely right."

She stood up, her movement fluid, purposeful. "Well, Benny, it looks like I'll be going now." She turned towards Franco, her lips curling into a faint, knowing smile. "And you, what was your name again? I'm not great with remembering names," she said with mock sweetness.

"Franco," he said, his eyes narrowing slightly as he studied her.

"Franco," Maria replied…... "I hope I never have to run into you again…..." With that, she turned and walked away, as Jessica followed close behind.

Once Maria left, Franco asked "Who is she?"

Benny, still tense, leaned in, lowering his voice as if the walls themselves could hear. "She's a rich bitch with a lot of connections," …... he said, glancing nervously. "So just steer clear of her, and you won't have any problems."

Franco's eyes fixed on Benny, processing the information. "And what? She is trouble?"

Benny nodded…., "She knows a lot of things. And she knows some very good cops. Trust me, you don't want to mess with her." ….. The warning was clear, as if Benny had spoken from bitter experience. He paused, his face turning darker. "She has power, and she doesn't use it lightly."

Franco sat back, something about Maria lingered in his mind—her confidence, the way she moved with purpose. She was not just some rich woman. There was more to her than that. But Benny was not finished…. "You saw her. She's dangerous in ways you don't even understand," Benny continued, his voice quieter now, almost hesitant, as if he did not want to say too much. At that moment, the phone rang. One of the employees picked it up, and a voice on the other end asked for Franco. It was his boss from Miami; the employee signalled to him, Franco walked over.

"What's going on, Franco?" the boss asked.

"Everything's going smoothly, boss. Everything's on track…" Franco replied.

"Any problems?" … The boss asked again.

"No, no problems, boss……" Franco continued… "Everything is fine. By tonight, we are on our way."

"Just be careful…." the boss continued…. "Tonight, everyone will be distracted watching the World Cup, so no mistakes. This is our golden ticket."

"Relax, boss. I will not slip up. I know what is at stake…" Franco said, reassuring his superior.

The line clicked dead as his boss hung up. Franco lowered the phone slowly, his mind already running through the plan again. Tonight had to be perfect.

That evening, the city felt electric, a huge day for all football fans. This year 1994, the FIFA World Cup, underway in the United States. It was the 10th of July, and the crowd in the local pub was buzzing with energy. On the big screen, the match between Bulgaria and Germany was unfolding, drawing everyone's attention. The pub door swung open, Maria entered, followed by Jessica. The moment Martin spotted them, his face lit up with a huge grin as he began making his way over.

"Hey… hey…come on…!" he cheered.

"Did it start already?" Maria asked, scanning the crowd.

"Yeah, it's already on…... Here, have a beer…..." Martin said, handing her a cold bottle. He glanced over at Jessica, then made a slightly funny/serious face.

"So, you found this one?" he said.

"Yeah, found her… for her luck…." Maria replied, her tone light but carrying an underlying tension.

So, all of them greeted each other and started watching the match. Germany took the lead, 1-0. Everyone rang with excitement. Not long after, a man came up to Jessica and whispered that someone outside had something good for her. She glanced at Maria, who was too absorbed in the game, went over to her and said she was heading to the bathroom. Jessica went outside, while inside, the tension was building as everyone waited to see if Bulgaria would equalise with a free kick.

And then, in the 75th minute, Hristo Stoichkov scored the equalizer with a direct free kick, and the score was 1-1. The entire place erupted in exhilaration. Just three minutes later, another Bulgarian player, Yordan Lechkov, scored the second goal, leading Bulgaria to a 2-1 victory over Germany. The crowd went wild with joy. But despite the excitement, Maria looked around and noticed that Jessica was still missing. She told Martin she was going to check on her and walked towards the bathroom. Realising Jessica wasn't there, Maria stepped outside, and just as she did, she saw a man pointing a gun at her.

As soon as Maria screamed, with urgency, she rushed towards them. The man, spotting her, turned and fired the gun. The bullet struck Jessica in the abdomen, sending her crashing to the ground in agony. After that, the man bolted, disappearing into the night, leaving Maria frozen in shock. She rushed to Jessica's side, her hands shaking as she tried to stop the bleeding, but it was clear the situation was dire.

The world around her seemed to blur. People inside the pub were still celebrating, oblivious to the horror that had just unfolded outside. Maria's heart pounded, her mind racing. She had to get Jessica help—now.

"Hold on, please, hold on...." Maria whispered frantically as she cradled Jessica's head in her lap. But the sound of footsteps approaching made her freeze. Would they make it in time?

By sheer chance, Martin stepped out of the pub just to witness the horror unfolding before him. He saw Maria kneeling beside Jessica, blood staining her clothes.

"Maria! What happened?" he shouted, rushing towards them.

"I don't know! They shot her! I don't know!" .... Maria cried out, panic rising in her voice. "Go, call an ambulance!"

Martin immediately called someone nearby to get help.

"It's going to be okay, just hold on!" .... Maria kept repeating, though the fear in her voice betrayed her reassurance.

"Maria!" .... Jessica gasped, her voice weak as she turned her head slightly, her eyes pleading.

"Don't talk, sweetheart, don't talk...." Martin urged, but Jessica's hand weakly grasped Maria's arm.

"No! Maria!" …. She whispered, her breath shallow, as she pulled Maria closer. Almost inaudibly, she leaned in and whispered directly into Maria's ear. "The address… save them! It's going to happen after midnight… save them! Save them!"

"What are you talking about?" …. Martin asked with confusion.

In that moment, Jessica took one final breath, her body going still in Maria's arms.

"Noooo! Noooo!" Maria screamed, her tears falling onto Jessica's limp form.

The ambulance arrived moments later, but it was too late. Jessica was gone. Martin pulled Maria into an embrace, holding her tightly, trying to steady her as the pressure of the situation crashed down on them.

"Maria… what did she mean? Who do you need to save?" ….. he asked with concern and desperation, but Maria could only shake her head, lost in the grief and the mystery of Jessica's last words.

She looked at him, her eyes sharp, like a quiet storm brewing. "I know who's behind this…." she said. Without waiting for his reaction, she pulled him aside, her hand gripping his arm tightly. "Listen very carefully…." she continued, her words cutting through the dread. "Go to my place. Get Ellie and Mikey. Bring them to your place. Keep them safe… for now."

Martin's brow furrowed, confusion and fear creeping in. "What? But what's happening?"

Maria didn't waste time. "Don't ask me. I don't have time for explanations. Just go……." Her tone was final, leaving no room for questions.

As she turned, her gaze locked onto a man leaving a bar across the street, his eyes glued to his phone. Without hesitation, Maria walked up to him, her movements precise, controlled. "Hey, I need your phone," she said, insistently.

The man looked up, startled. "But hey, wait!"

"I don't want to be rude," Maria cut him off, her smile tight. "Thanks for the help." With that, she snatched the phone from his hand before he could protest.

She dialled the number with speed, her fingers moving like a machine. The phone rang, on the other end, a voice answered-Hannah, the police chief busy in her kitchen, the sound of sizzling food barely audible in the background.

"Hannah, listen. I'm sending you an address…... It's urgent……I need you to gather as many people as you can and get there. Do it fast."

Hannah's voice was filled with confusion and concern…... "Maria? Is that you? What's going on? What address? What the hell is happening?"

Maria's eyes darkened as she glanced around the street, her mind racing with thoughts of who might be listening. "I don't have time to explain…. Just trust me. Get your team, and come to…" She hesitated for a moment, lowering her voice as if speaking the address would bring danger closer. The name of the location hung for a second, unspoken, a secret only meant for those in the know.

"Alright…" Hannah replied, she walked quickly to her husband, explaining she had to leave for an urgent operation.

Maria handed the phone back to the man with a simple, quiet thank you. But her eyes quickly moved to the motorbike beside him. "Is this yours too?" she asked.

He hesitated, clearly thinking about it, and then said, "Don't you dare!"

Maria didn't wait for his permission. In one smooth motion, she swung her leg over the motorbike and fired it up. The engine roared to life, cutting through the cold evening.

The man froze, his face darkening with anger. "Oh no… no, no, you're not taking my motorbike too," he exclaimed, watching her drive off.

As she sped away, he stood there for a moment, seething, before muttering through clenched teeth, "What's wrong with women these days? Taking whatever they want… and then they complain there are no real men…." His frustration echoed in the silence.

Maria arrived at the designated address, her eyes scanning the area as she parked a little distance away. The lot stretched out before her—massive, filled with more than forty towering trucks, their bulk casting long shadows under the dim light. The engines hummed low, a steady, almost eerie background noise. The smell of diesel and metal filled the air, mixing with the quiet buzz of activity. Everything here felt… heavy.

She moved closer, staying low, her footsteps muffled by the concrete. As she approached, she spotted Franco and Benny talking in the distance, their voices low, too far to hear clearly over the hum. But she wasn't alone for long. From among the shadows, a guard emerged, flanked with a group of burly men, their presence more felt than seen. One of them grabbed Maria by the arm, spinning her toward Franco, gun raised to her head.

"Boss," one-off the guards said "Look who we found lurking around."

Franco barely glanced at her, his expression unreadable. "Well, well," he said, carrying no surprise, just a quiet amusement.

Benny's eyes narrowed, his posture strong. "I told you not to get involved with her," he said sharply.

Franco's eyes met Bennys', annoyance flaring. "Benny," he said, "You're starting to get on my nerves." Without another word, his finger tightened on the trigger. A single shot rang out, echoing through the parking lot. Benny fell silent, his body crumpling to the ground like a broken doll.

Turning to the rest of the men, Franco spoke with quiet finality. "Take care of her. Get rid of the body."

"Do you know..." Maria started, something purposeful in her words.

Franco turned slowly, the shift in his expression subtle but telling. "What?"

"He was right," she said, her eyes locking onto his.

"Right about what?" His impatience was now palpable, his hand twitching near his weapon.

"Right to be afraid," Maria replied, but before he could react, she moved quick. In an instant, she snatched the guard's gun, pressing it against his head, then using him as cover as she spun, in one fluid motion.

The sound of a shot fired, sharp and precise. Maria hadn't aimed to kill—no. It was for Franco's hand, the one holding the weapon. He staggered back, eyes wide in shock as his gun dropped to the ground.

Maria shifted her focus. Her aim was flawless, each shot fired with purpose—as each man fell, crippled but not dead. She shot them in the hands, in the legs—just enough to disable them, to strip them of their ability to fight back. The scene was chaotic, but it was calculated. She moved like lightning, her body sliding between trucks for cover, her eyes scanning for the next target.

"Move! Move!" Franco barked in Portuguese; filled with fury. The rest of his men scrambled, diving into the trucks, engines roaring as they tried to flee.

Maria darted out from behind the steel walls of the trucks, but she was not done. She had no intention of letting them escape. Just as the first lorry began to roll, the unmistakable sound of sirens screamed in the distance, fast, too fast. The trucks' tires screeched as they tried to push forward, but the road was blocked— police had arrived, and there was no way out. The escape route had vanished.

Maria stayed low, her heart racing, knowing that this fight was far from over.

"Finally," Maria muttered under her breath as the police stormed in. After a couple of seconds, the criminals were on the ground, hands behind their heads. When Franco saw what was happening, his eyes went wild. Before anyone could stop him, he moved the pistol to his own head, pulling the trigger. The sharp sound of the shot rang through the scene, leaving the crowd in stunned silence.

The officers began opening all the massive truck doors. And then, the truth came crumbling down. The trucks, full of what they thought were supplies, were instead packed with people—suffering, trapped, desperate.

Maria's mind raced as she approached Franco's lifeless body; her thoughts locked in a whirl of unanswered questions.

"I can't believe it, Maria," Hannah said urgently. "This... this is a massive human trafficking ring……. How did you know?"

Maria didn't look at her. Her eyes were still fixed on Franco, her mind working overtime. "I don't know…..." she replied slowly. "But something doesn't add up. He wouldn't have killed himself for this. Something bigger is happening here."

Hannah stepped closer, her concern deepening. "How did you know? What made you suspect it?"

Maria's gaze shifted, piercing. "The real question isn't how I knew. It's where this is coming from... and where these people are being taken. You need to gather intel—how much time do you need?"

Her words were precise, the answers just out of reach. The mystery deepened with every second.

Hannah gave Maria a reassuring glance before responding, "Don't worry, when we have something new, I'll make sure to tell you right away." She paused, catching sight of the troubled scene with the policemen, and began to organise everything, taking control of the situation as best as she could.

Chapter 2

Months later, things were calmer. Maria and Martin continued running the homeless restaurant, helping those in need...... One evening, as Maria was serving, she noticed Martin signalling for her to come over. She walked up to him, wiping her hands on her apron, "What's up?" she asked, sensing something on his mind.

"Is everything, okay?" she asked, noticing how serious he looked.

Martin smiled, though there was a hint of nervousness. "Yeah, everything's fine. Just wondering if it'd be alright if I leave early today. Ellie, Mikey and I... we've got plans."

Maria blinked, processing what he said. "Ellie and Mikey?" she asked, a smile moving onto her face as it clicked. "So... you and Ellie...?" Her eyes softened, full of surprise and warmth.

Martin looked slightly flustered but nodded, a smile cracking through. "Yeah, it's been a while now. We've found something special together."

Maria placed a hand on his shoulder. "Well, I'm happy for you both. Tell Ellie I said hi, and give Mikey a big hug for me. Go on, don't keep them waiting."

Martin laughed, relieved by her response. "Thanks, Maria.Take care of the restaurant." He turned to go but stopped, looking back at her with a smile. "Thanks for understanding."

Just before leaving the restaurant, he saw Maria carrying a large tray of empty plates, and without meaning to, she dropped them on the ground. The noise startled everyone around her, and the customers' faces tensed as they watched how the plates shattered into pieces. Maria, slightly embarrassed but trying to keep her cool, quickly bent down to clean up the mess. She mumbled to herself, "Classic, Maria, classic."

Martin couldn't help but laugh. He looked at her with a smirk. "You're always getting into trouble, aren't you?"

Maria looked up, chuckling sheepishly as she picked up the shards. "I swear, I don't mean to. It just happens."

Martin shook his head, still smiling. "Okay, okay, I'm going now, but you keep doing you. You're good at it." He winked and waved as he headed out, calling back, "Take care of this place, Maria!"

She watched him leave, her face flushing slightly from the little mishap, but also feeling a sense of warmth. Despite the mess, everything felt… right. She stood up, took a deep breath, and finished tidying up, her usual clumsy charm still shining through as the restaurant returned to its normal bustle.

After finishing work, Maria stepped outside, the rain already starting to fall gently. She stretched her arms wide, closed her eyes, and let the soft drizzle kiss her face. Her movements were graceful, like an actress playing a quiet, tender scene—effortless and serene. She wasn't concerned with what others thought; she was simply embraced in the moment. The world around her—the fresh scent of rain, the soft rustle of trees—felt like a symphony, and she was part of it all.

People passing by her on the street started taking out their umbrellas and looked at her strangely, one woman even said something aloud… "Wow, she's crazy!" Maria, unfazed, smiled softly and thought to herself, "Hmm, rather freer… but everyone has their opinion."

She returned to her apartment, drenched but glowing with happiness. She quickly changed, made herself a warm cup of tea, and went to the window. From there, she watched the street below, where a little child and an elderly man, probably the child's grandfather, were happily playing together in the rain. The rain had eased, just a light drizzle now, but it didn't stop them. The man was laughing as he watched the child jump through puddles, and the child's laughter rang out with pure joy. Maria smiled at the sight, feeling the simplicity and beauty of the moment.

She sat by the window for a while, letting the peaceful scene wash over her. The steady rhythm of the rain and the warmth of the moment gently lulled her into a deep, contented sleep, while the world outside continued its quiet dance in the rain.

It was already evening, and Maria found herself trapped in a strange dream. She was walking down a narrow street when she heard someone calling a name, "Gloria! Gloria! Come here, you silly child!" Startled, she turned, but the street had changed. It was bright and sunny now, bustling with life, people passing by. A child ran past, clearly escaping from an old woman. But when Maria looked at the old woman, her heart stopped. "Grandma!" she whispered, almost choking on the word, her voice shaking as she lowered her head. And then, she raised her eyes, her heart heavy with confusion. "What am I dreaming?" she thought, overwhelmed by the surreal feeling.

In that instant, the old woman was standing right in front of her. "Yes, you're dreaming," the woman said softly. Maria couldn't breathe for a moment. It was her grandmother, her warm, comforting grandmother. With a gentle wave of her hand, they both found themselves back in their old home, sitting by the fireplace, the warmth wrapping around them. The familiar smell of tea filled the space.

"You've learned how to control your dreams!" her grandmother said.

"Not fully," Maria whispered, "but I'm trying." Her eyes welled up, as she could barely hold back the flood of emotion. "I miss you so much… I miss you so much, Grandma!"

Her grandmother's eyes softened. "Would you like some tea?" she asked.

"Yes," Maria managed to say, her words fragile. Her grandmother nodded, a silent understanding passing between them, and gestured to the table where a cup of tea awaited her. Maria took it with shaking hands, her fingers barely able to hold the cup as tears began to spill. She sipped it, but her gaze never left her grandmother's face, her eyes filled with desperate longing.

"I have so many questions," Maria said.

Her grandmother leaned in, her face full of compassion. "Now's not the time for questions, my dear," she said gently, the sounds wrapping around Maria like a soft embrace. "You need to be strong as difficult times are coming for you. Always remember— no one is without fault."

Maria's heart broke, every word sinking deep into her soul. She wanted to hold on to this moment forever, even though she knew it wasn't real. She closed her eyes, tears streaming down her face, feeling both the emotion of the dream and the love that never truly left.

And so, her grandmother continued, her voice soft, as though every word was carefully chosen, meant to soothe and hold meaning. "People in this world make many mistakes, and they keep making them because they believe it's the only way to find safety, the only way to survive."

Maria's chest tightened, she whispered, "I know, Grandma. The world isn't a war. We make the war. We make the rules. We create our own world."

Her grandmother looked at her with eyes full of understanding, the kind only a grandmother could give. "But sometimes," Maria's voice faltered, "it's so hard to show the good of people, the side they don't even want to see."

Her grandmother nodded, a slight sadness in her eyes. "Because everyone has their own choice, my dear. Everyone chooses who they want to be, and who they will remain. But most people bury their inner voice, their beauty, because they feel they have to become what everyone expects them to be."

Maria wished she could hold onto this moment, the soft sadness of it all, but it slipped through her fingers like water. She needed her grandmother's wisdom now more than ever, yet it felt so far away.

"I know, and that's why I don't judge, Grandma," Maria whispered……

"Everyone is what they believe themselves to be. I'm just happy to be myself, thanks to you."

As she spoke these words, Maria struggled to hold back her tears, feeling a mixture of gratitude and sorrow.

Her grandmother's eyes softened, and she gently spoke, "My dear…" Her voice was warm, but there was a hint of sadness in it, too. She rose slowly, reaching out with her hands, as if she had something important to say. She touched Maria's face, a gesture that felt like a quiet blessing. Maria held her hand tightly, as if it were the only thing anchoring her to this moment. Then, through the veil of her tears, she kissed her grandmother's hand, overcome with the wave of emotions she couldn't keep inside anymore.

"I am not the reason for you to be yourself, my dear," her grandmother said.

"You are the reason. All I did was show you that there's no point in jealousy, greed, judgment, or hate. People forget that we're all part of one big family, that we are all one. Because of this, as we grow, we start hurting one another just to have more than the other. But you, you are who you are, as the choice is yours. You have always had the choice."

Maria's heart clenched as her grandmother's words sparked in her mind. She took a deep breath before speaking, "Yes, we can't help those who don't want to help themselves first…" Her thoughts wandered to Jessica, the meaning of those words suddenly making more sense.

"Exactly," her grandmother said, quiet and knowing, she had always understood the unspoken struggles Maria carried.

"Now I understand, Grandma," Maria whispered. She couldn't help but think of Jessica again, and the conflict she carried with her.

Her grandmother's gaze softened, "I know, my dear. You always try to understand."

The silence between them stretched, telling and worthwhile, then her grandmother spoke again.

"Be ready," she said.

"Ready for what?" Maria's voice faltered, unsure if she wanted to know the answer.

However, before her grandmother could respond, a thunderous clap of lightning tore through the stillness of the dream. Maria's eyes shot open, her heart pounding in her chest, as if the storm had followed her into the waking world. She rushed to close the window, but her thoughts were still tangled in the conversation. The dream had slipped away, leaving only the residue of its emotional weight.

She stood there for a moment, breathless, trying to understand what had just happened, as the storm raged on outside. What did her grandmother mean? And why did it feel like the answer was so close, yet still out of her reach?

The next morning, Maria headed to the police station, her thoughts heavy. It had been too long without any updates from Hannah about the case. No calls—just silence. A strange kind of silence that made her restless. As she walked in, she took out a sandwich from her bag and began unwrapping it. Just as she was about to take a bite, she caught sight of one of the detainees. His eyes lingered on the sandwich, a quiet plea in his expression.

Maria paused, then handed it to him without a word.

"Make sure he gets more food and water," she told one of the officers.

Without waiting for a response, she asked where Hannah was. When they directed her to the office, Maria walked in to find Hannah on the phone. The tone of her voice was sharp and controlled—until she noticed Maria.

Hannah ended the call quickly, her expression unreadable.

"Maria," she said cautiously. "I wasn't expecting you to stop by."

"Well, let's say I came to check on you since I haven't heard anything from you, and it's been quite a while. But why is there still nothing on this case? Maria asked.

We can't find anything—no leads on who's behind it," Hannah said.

"What about this Franco?" Maria added.

"The strange thing about Franco is that there's nothing—nothing at all about him. It's like he doesn't exist. His file's empty. Everything's blank," Hannah said, gesturing to his wallet, she handed it over to Maria.

Maria took the wallet, flipping it open. It was empty, just as Hannah had described. As her eyes lingered on the interior, something caught her attention—a small card tucked away inside. She pulled it out, turning it over. It wasn't a business card. It was a night club card, the kind you'd get if you were a regular.

"What is this?" Hannah asked, her gaze fixed.

Maria stared at the words "Albanian Oriental Club", a Miami nightclub. A strange unease settled in her thighs. That can't be... she thought, but she quickly pushed it aside. There was no reason for it to affect her this way.

"I think... this is from Miami," Maria said, though something in her expression hinted at a hidden layer. She handed the card to Hannah.

Hannah glanced at it, peaking interest.

Maria tried to stay composed, but her mind kept circling. Something about that card felt wrong, yet she couldn't put her finger on why. She shifted slightly, hiding the uncertainty. The question lingered—Why does this feel so familiar? — but Maria didn't say a word.

Maria deliberately knocked the glass of water onto the floor.

"Oh, sorry, Hannah!" she said, stepping back as if it were an accident.

"No, Maria, the carpet's new!" Hannah said, rushing to check the spill. While Hannah was focused on the mess, she left the card on the table. Maria quickly snatched it without Hannah noticing, muttered a quick "Bye," and hurried out.

Down on the street, she walked to a phone booth. She dialled a number, once she had finished, she stared at the card in her hand, her focus sharpening.

She waited.

"Come on, come on, pick up the phone, Lee", she thought. She didn't need to be nervous—she just needed him to answer. Her fingers tapped lightly on the booth's receiver, but her eyes remained fixed on the card. The phone number was for the Miami police station. At that moment, one of the secretaries heard the phone ringing. She reached to pick it up, but before her hand could touch the receiver, another hand gently stopped her.

It was John, Lee's nephew. A tall, broad-shouldered man with striking light hair, he had the kind of presence that made heads turn. His smile was effortless, disarming. His piercing blue eyes held a quiet confidence, yet there was an undeniable warmth about him. He wasn't just a pretty face—John was known for his sharp instincts and cool demeanour, especially in high-pressure situations.

He was one of those rare types—a charming guy who could handle any situation, whether it required a smile or a stern command.

"Sarah, who told you that you have the right to touch Uncle's phone?" John teased.

He gave the secretary a reassuring look before calmly taking the phone. "I've got it," he said.

"Oh, come on, John!" Sarah laughed, glancing at the phone that wouldn't stop ringing. "This thing's been ringing off the hook, and you're not picking up?" she said, her voice playful as she reached for the receiver.

John smirked. "Relax, I'll take it from here. You go make me a nice coffee."

Sarah gave him a mischievous look, her smile widening. "Oh, how could I possibly say no to you?" she teased, her tone light and flirtatious. "I mean, you know I can't, right?"

With a playful wink, Sarah left to make the coffee as John calmly picked up the phone, his smirk never fading.

"Hello, hello, John on the phone, how can I help you?"

"Hello, hello," Maria started to speak. "I would like to speak with Inspector Jin Wang."

"That's not possible, ma'am. But you can talk to me, I'm his nephew, John Wang. Go ahead, I'm listening."

Maria placed the receiver against her chest confused, muttering to herself, "His nephew?" Strange. She thought for a moment." Maybe now his nephew is living with him? Could it be?" she thought in her mind.

She quickly returned the receiver to her ear. "Look, sir, I really don't have time to explain. It's very important. Could I speak to Lee?"

"Lee?" John's tone shifted immediately. He suddenly became serious. Only those closest to him called him by that name.

"Ma'am… my uncle has been dead for almost a year now."

"Dead?" Maria froze, stunned. She slowly lowered the receiver, her mind racing.

But it seems you were close…John continued. "Tell me what you need, and I'll help you."

"Ma'am, are you still there?" John asked, but there was no answer. Maria had already hung up.

John stood there looking at his uncle's phone in disbelief. Someone had just been asking about him. He couldn't help but wonder who this was.

"Here's your coffee, John," Sarah said, setting a cup on the table.

"What's going on? Who was that on the phone?" she asked.

"I don't know, but… could you check the origin of the call?" John said.

"Yeah, sure," she said, a faint worry creeping into her mind.

As evening fell, Martin and Ellie had just finished setting the table for dinner when the doorbell rang. Martin opened the door, surprised to find Maria standing there.

"Maria!" he exclaimed. "Good evening, Martin," she replied, stepping inside. But as she entered, Martin and Ellie couldn't help but notice something was off about her. She seemed distant, a little lost in thought.

Mikey, as if sensing her unease, rushed over and jumped into her lap. He nuzzled her gently, smiling as she stroked his hair. Slowly, a calm seemed to wash over her. She sighed, her expression softening. With Mikey there, everything seemed to settle back into place.

Meanwhile, in Miami, John returned to his apartment. He plopped into the chair, taking his cat into his arms. The phone rang, but he didn't answer. He just sat there, the cat in his lap, staring at the device. The voicemail light blinked.

He listened carefully as Sarah's voice filled the silence.

"Hi, John! Looks like you're still not home. The number you asked me to trace. Well, I found out where it's from. It's from a phone booth in Manchester, UK. It could be someone close to your uncle, or maybe someone doesn't know that he's passed away. I hope this information helps. Have a nice evening, John!"

John was confused. He walked over to the cabinet in the living room, filled with family photos. Picking up a picture of himself and his uncle, he studied it closely.

"Manchester... Hmmm... Uncle Lee... Interesting... Very interesting," he muttered to himself. Then, setting the photo back in its place, he headed to take a shower.

Elsewhere, Maria's conversation with Martin had already started. Now, alone in the kitchen, she had told him exactly what she was planning to do.

"Are you sure?" Martin asked uncertainly.

"Yes, Martin. Relax. Don't worry about me," Maria reassured him. "I'll be gone for a while, but I have to go. This person was really close to me."

"He… passed away?" Martin hesitated.

"Yes" Maria admitted. "I just wish I had one more chance to see him."

"Yeah… When we lose someone, we always wish for another moment. But we don't get one, do we?" Martin sighed. "It's cruel."

Maria gave him a knowing smile, letting out a quiet sigh as she patted his shoulder. She turned to leave, but Martin stopped her.

"Maria, wait! "Why does it feel like you're saying goodbye? Is there something you're not telling me?"

"Martin, everything's fine. And everything will stay under control. Don't worry." She smiled again, but this time, it was different. "Just take care of yourself, and Ellie, and the little one too." She paused, then added, "Keep the business running. I'm leaving everything to you because I trust you. You're a good man. I'm really grateful to know you—to have you in my life as a friend."

Martin let out a short laugh, but there was no humour in it. "Oh, come on. Stop it. What's going on, Maria? This… this sounds like a real goodbye." He took a step closer, his expression darkening. "Tell me the truth, because right now, you're starting to scare me."

Maria turned slightly, and without meaning to, knocked over a glass, which shattered on the floor. Both of them jumped, surprised.

"Oh, sorry!" Maria said, laughing a little.

"No worries, Maria. It's just a glass. By the way, I've hidden the good ones in the cupboard above, far away from you."

"What? Seriously?" she added.

They both laughed, the tension easing between them.

"Don't worry about me, Martin. Just trust me. That's all I need," she said, and gave him one last look before turning to leave.

Chapter 3

The next morning, at the Miami police station, John had just arrived at work when he noticed one of the officers yelling at a teenager, a criminal in cuffs. He walked over and asked,

"Hey, hey, what's going on here?"

"This little punk thinks he's something special," the officer growled.

"At least I'm not like you, fat and stupid," the teenager retorted with a smirk.

"Whoa, whoa, take it easy," John said to the officer as he stepped in to diffuse the situation. He turned to the teenager. "So, you think you're pretty tough?" he asked.

"What now? You gonna give me a lesson in manners?" the teenager asked dismissively.

"Why would I give you a lesson in manners?" John replied, his voice calm.

"Who am I to do that? Your life is yours, and you choose how to live it. But I guess, since you're too lazy to become organised and take control, you choose the effortless way to destroy your life. From what I see, you don't even have the intention to fight for it. So go ahead, spend your best years in prison," John said, turning to leave.

But the teenager stopped him, his voice tinged with sadness. "You don't get it. My life isn't that easy."

John turned back and looked him straight in the eye.

"No, you don't get it. No one's life is that easy. I grew up on the streets in Brazil. I lost my mother when I was a kid. Then my father. And a year ago, I lost my uncle. So, no matter what life throws at you, and no matter how nasty people are to you, you choose whether to be just like them—an asshole to others—or if you'll try to be something better for yourself."

With that, John turned and walked away, speaking a few final word's hoping he would think about them…. "The choice is yours to make."

And then, just seconds later, someone played Selena's "Buddy, Buddy, Boom, Boom," encouraging everyone to start to dance. As their officer of the month, John walked in. Everyone was in high spirits, enjoying the moment.

People admired John, especially his dream of believing in the law and always being fair. Some of them whispered, "What more does a guy like him need? He needs to find a good woman, and that's all. Nothing else matters. Just look at him."

By that time, Maria had already arrived in Miami. As she stepped out of the airport, she looked around, paused for a moment, took a deep breath, and whispered to herself "here we go again!"

She then hailed a taxi, got in, and they drove off. She told the driver to turn up the music, the same Selena song was playing.

"So, you like Selena?" the driver asked her in Spanish.

"Of course, I love her. Who doesn't like Selena?" she replied in Spanish.

"Aha, I knew it, you're Spanish," he said.

"No, actually, I'm not, but I speak many languages," she answered.

"Well, where are we headed?" he asked.

"Drive, I'll tell you" She said.

Soon enough, they arrived at the cemetery. The taxi driver stopped, turned to her, and said in Spanish, "Here? Girl, you don't belong here…… beautiful!"

Maria smiled softly and said, "Yes, but one day we all will. Death doesn't choose." She paused for a moment. "She's for everyone," she told him, and then left.

She walked over to the gravestone of her grandmother. Carrying only a single red rose with her. Placing it gently on the grave, the inscription on the gravestone reading, Camilla and Gloria de Perez, born in 1926, 1967, and died in1989.

Beneath it, there was another inscription: "Life is a ladder we must climb, not something we stand still on". And "always be the best version of yourself, for yourself."

Maria gently caressed the gravestone from top to bottom, smiled warmly, closed her eyes for a moment, and then stood up, sighing deeply, as she walked away.

As the sun set, Maria was standing in a phone booth. She looked at the business card in her hand and waited for someone to pick up the phone. At the police station, John was about to leave, saying goodbye to everyone, walking over to his desk to grab his jacket. He picked it up and was about to head out when his uncle's phone rang again. He looked at it, puzzled, and answered.

"Hello, John on the phone. How can I help you?"

"Hey, John," Maria's voice came through the line.

"I need you to listen carefully, this is important," she said.

John was confused, adding... "You're the one who called the other day, right?"

"Yes." Maria replied.

She hesitated, a brief pause, a deep breath. "I can't talk to your uncle. But I think I can trust you."

John's interest sharpened. "I'm listening."

By eight in the evening, Maria told him, "You'll gather your best people and come to...", giving him the address and some information.

He was shocked as he repeated it. "This is a serious accusation, and this information... Where did you get all this from?"

"Just be there at the time, at the place I told you. Don't ask any more questions. And do what I tell you. Don't tell anyone," She said.

He hesitated, disbelief showing on his face. "You think everyone will follow me without a word? Why? I don't even know you—you are just telling me what to do."

Maria continued. "Let's just say, there is a connection between us—your uncle. That's what ties us. And if you want more answers, you'll come"

He stood there, still processing her words, unsure. "And what about you? Who are you, really?"

Before he could get another word out, the line went dead.

John, still holding the phone, stood frozen, his thoughts racing.

Meanwhile, Maria was already heading towards the Albanian club—the one she found the address to on the card in Franco's wallet.

Inside, oriental music was playing. Maria started looking around, and everywhere there were oriental dancers. She entered discreetly and unnoticed, wearing a red top, a jacket, and jeans. Her hair was tied up with a few curls falling loose.

One of the dancers began to take Maria's jacket off, moving to the rhythm of the music, while another dancer came and removed the rest, leaving her in just her top. The owner of the establishment noticed and approached her. He was an Albanian man, around fifty years old, with a gold chain around his neck.

"Hello," he said.

"Hello," she replied.

"What is a beautiful girl like you doing here?" he asked.

"There are many beautiful girls here," she responded,

The owner looked at her with intrigue. "Do you want to be more than just one of them?

"Actually, I do," she said.

"Good. Come to my office. We will talk," he said.

And together, they left, moving upstairs.

They both headed up to his office with bodyguards trailing behind. Entering, they had a clear view of everything below, the boss took a seat at his desk. Maria sat across from him, the guards standing silently behind her.

"Alright, show me what you've got," he challenged, Maria glanced at the guards, then back at him, her expression serious.

"I can do a lot," she replied. "But I need to show you everything in private."

The guards exchanged a look, as he nodded at them to leave.

"Fine," he said. Once they were alone, Maria stood up, walked over, and locked the door, making it clear they would not be interrupted.

Maria leaned closer, fixing her gaze on him. With a playful yet gentle manner, she started to tease him lightly. Then, taking his hands, she placed them gently on the chair's arms and secured them with soft rope she pulled from her pockets.

He smiled, intrigued. "What is this? A game?" he asked, a playful sparkle in his eyes.

Maria leaned closer, her eyes locked onto his. Smiling, she reached out and, in a swift motion, touched the back of his neck with her finger. The touch was so quick and precise that he instantly froze, unable to move. She had effectively found the pressure point, making him paralysed.

Maria paced the room before walking over to the window, glancing down at the bar below.

"Do you know what acupuncture points are? … Therapeutic points? … Or self-defence pressure points? ".. she asked purposefully.

After a moment, she pulled up a chair and sat across from him, continuing her explanation with the same steady intensity.

"Acupuncture points are connected to the body's meridians—the pathways through which life energy, Chi energy, flows," Maria explained.

"In Chinese medicine, applying pressure to these points can influence certain organs or even relieve pain."

"Therapeutic points? Those are gentle. Massage therapists use them to relax muscles, ease tension… help people feel at peace.

But pressure points for self-defense?" A sly grin. "Now those... those can-do real damage."

The grip tightens, she continued. "In the right hands, a little pressure in just the right place can shut down your body. Cut off your movement. Turn pleasure into a weapon. Right now, you're struggling because your brain isn't getting enough blood. Stay like this too long, and—boom." A pause, almost amused. "Like a bomb going off in your head."

"So, here is how this goes. I ask. You answer. Then I walk away. But if you think about calling security?" The pressure sharpens— just enough to prove a point. "We do this again. And next time? I let you pop."

She moved closer and ask him "So, are you in?"

Then she chuckled softly and added, "Ha, but look at me. I'm asking you like you can give me the answer. Of course, you can't answer me."

With a quick, deliberate motion, she released him, settling back into her chair across from him. He gasped for air, his eyes wide with fear, and asked, "Damn it, who are you?"

She leaned forward slightly, a cold smirk appearing on her lips.

"I don't have an answer for that." She paused, letting the words hang in the air.

"But I'm the one asking the questions. I'm the one who will get the answers, not the other way around."

Her gaze sharpened. "So, let's get started. And don't even think about lying to me, because today, I'm in the mood. Who knows? I might press the wrong spot without meaning to, and then I'll just walk away."

She fixed him with a hard stare. "Now, tell me. Do you know a Franco? This business card was found in his wallet. It's your bar, isn't it?"

He glanced at the card, then back into her eyes, his fear unmistakable.

"No, I don't know anyone by that name, I don't know him," he said nervously.

"Is that so?" she asked, skeptical.

She leaned in slightly, her gaze intense. "Let me make it clearer. I know exactly who you are and what you are involved in."

Her focus shifted to his desk, where a photo of his wife and two daughters sat. She pointed at the picture. "I know you don't realise it, but this..." She gestured to the photo. "This is the meaning of your life, not what's happening here."

He glanced at the photo and then back at her. "Don't you dare," he muttered.

"I will not do anything to your family.... You have already done enough to them." she said.

"I don't think you want this life for your daughters, do you?" she asked him, looking deep into his eyes

He stayed silent, and she nodded, as if confirming her thoughts. "I thought so."

Her gaze hardened as she continued, "But the sad truth is, people like you, who turn off their conscience and don't care about what happens to the people around them, end up being selfish. If someone touched your family, you would react—because they are your family. But to people like you, everyone else is just a number. They are people who have also shut off their conscience, who don't care about anything except their own selfishness…. And you know…" she paused… "Without even realising it, people like you become exactly what they hate. As the ones they despise the most… are the ones who have hurt them the most."

She tilted her head slightly, watching him. "There are two choices. The easy one…. Become just like them. The hard one…...Well … it's to be different. But for most people, that's nearly impossible."

She lowered her gaze to her watch. Her finger hovered over the glass face as she counted—slowly, deliberately.

"Five…" A glance at him.

"Four…" A measured breath.

"Three…" The tension in the room building.

"Two…" The faintest smirk played at her lips.

"One."

The alarm blared. The sound shattered the silence, sharp and unrelenting. He flinched, eyes darting around, confusion flashing across his face. She exhaled, almost amused. "Right now," she said smoothly, "the police are tearing through your little hidden dirty business."

She let the words hit him before adding, "You're right under this club."

Beneath the bar was a massive underground arena for illegal fights, with massive illegal bets taking place. The police team rushed in quickly, and while everyone was in shock, most could not escape.

"But how? How did you know?" the Albanian boss asked.

"I know a lot of things," she replied, cool and steady.

There was a knock at the door—security.

Maria glared at the Albanian boss. Before he could yell for help, she swiftly touched his neck. He collapsed, unconscious. She moved to the door, opened it. The two guards stormed in, about to ask what was going on. In the same smooth motion, she touched both their necks, and they, too, fell silent. Just before lowering them gently to the ground, she whispered, "Sleep."

She looked down the corridor, but it was pure chaos. People running in every direction. She waited, letting the frenzy die down. When the hall cleared, Maria slipped out. Just as the door closed behind her, a voice shouted from the end of the corridor, "Stop! Don't move!"

She turned to face him. It was John, but she had no idea who he was. He did not recognise her either—the woman from the phone.

"I don't have time for this," she told him.

"Oh, really?" he said, stepping toward her, his gun pointed.

"I don't think so," he told her.

"Seriously, I don't have time for this," she replied. Before he even realised it, she had snatched the gun from his grip and aimed it at him.

"I told you—I really don't have time for this," she repeated.

John stared at her, stunned by how quickly she had disarmed him, before he could react, Maria's head tilted. In the distance, down the corridor, figures were moving toward them, guards. Without hesitation, she grabbed John by the shoulder and yanked him down behind her. Then, with precise aim, she fired two quick shots. The bullets struck the guards' hands, knocking their weapons away and sending them crashing to the floor. John saw his chance. He lunged for a gun nearby, but Maria was faster. In one fluid motion, she switched her pistol from her right hand to her left and aimed it directly at him.

"Don't even think about it," she warned.

She kicked the gun out of his reach just as voices rang out from the other end of the corridor. More officers were arriving, shouting at the downed guards to stay put.

Maria did not stick around. She quickly dismantled John's gun, tossed the useless pieces to the floor, and disappeared.

The officers rushed, helping John up. "What the hell happened?" one of them demanded as they pulled him up. Without waiting for an answer, they walked toward the office. Inside, they found the two guards' unconscious—and their boss slumped in his chair, wrists locked behind him in handcuffs.

One officer knelt to check for a pulse. "They're alive," he confirmed. "Just out cold."

John said nothing. He could still feel the energy of Maria's gun aimed at him, the speed, the precision, and for the first time in a while he felt a spark, something unfamiliar. One of the officers looked at John and smirked. "Well, this is interesting, John. Looks like the guy who gave you that information really did his job well."

The other officer chuckled. "With this much evidence, that guy's not walking out of prison anytime soon."

They looked at the club owner, still slumped in the chair, cuffed and silent. But John was not paying attention. He stood there, deep in thought, not saying a word.

Chapter 4

Back at the police station, the whole place was buzzing. Officers were busy processing the criminals caught at the club, everyone too occupied to focus on anything else.

John's friend approached him. "The boss of the club is awake," he said.

John headed straight for the interrogation room. Stepping inside, he placed the man's file on the table and sat down.

"Let's talk," he said.

"Well, how is it going? It has been a while," John said as he flipped open the file, scanning the pages. He didn't even remember the guy's name.

"Ah… Mr. Boran Fadil," he read aloud. Then he looked up.

"Not sure if you realise this, but after everything we found—especially in your office—things aren't looking too good for you."

He leaned back slightly…. "If you ask me… I do not think you are walking out of here anytime soon."

Boran's eyes stared at John. "I want to talk to my lawyer."

John leaned back…. "Oh, of course you do"

"But you already know he will not help you. You're not stupid. The only thing that might work in your favour is if you cooperate—if you give me something useful." He said.

Boran didn't blink. Instead, he leaned in, his voice dropping…. "Do you know her?"

John's expression didn't change…. "Who should I know?"

Boran pulled back, laughing under his breath…. "Ah… playing dumb, huh? Your friend—she knows too much."

John's jaw tightened… "If you mean the woman, I don't know her."

Boran studied him for a moment before shaking his head…

"Strange," he muttered. "No one knew her. I never thought I'd meet her."

He exhaled slowly; his demeanour was heavier now— real.

"Five years ago, we went underground. No one even dared to breathe too loud because of her. She didn't come after small fish like us… she pulled bigger ones down with her. Some of them were yours—from your own department." Boran said, a serious look on his face.

John held his gaze, his mind working through the implications, but Boran was not finished.

"You know…" His voice dropped lower, almost as if he were confessing something he had not even admitted to himself before. "Five years ago, I didn't have kids."

He faltered, just for a second, before letting out a bitter chuckle. Then, he wiped at his eye, as if the tear had no business being there in the first place.

"I had nothing back then. Just the job, the money, the rush of it all. And I thought that was enough."

His expression hardened again, but there was something different in his eyes now—something rawer. He looked straight at John.

"You do not realise what matters until it's too late. You don't get to go back and fix it." He said to himself.

"I can help you," John said.

Boran shook his head slowly. "The fact is, no one can help me," he replied. "One way or another, they will find a way to erase me. I'm finished."

He spoke again, the gravity of his words pressing. "But if you promise to help my family or at least give them a fresh start somewhere far away, I'll tell you things—things that are far more serious than you can imagine."

John looked at him interested, and serious… "I'll do everything I can to protect them," he promised.

Boran looked at him, his expression hardening.

"A storm's coming," he began. "We have a new boss. Someone pulling the strings so well that no one dares to oppose him. Your friend's been asking about Franco."

"Who's this Franco?" John asked, his curiosity piqued.

Boran let out a quiet laugh, then fixed John with a piercing stare.

"You do not know who Franco is? But you know who I am? That means you know nothing," Boran said, with a mix of mockery and warning.

"Then start talking," John said. "Do your part, and I'll do mine."

Boran nodded… "Alright, about a month and a half ago, there was a big operation in the UK, in Manchester. It was well-planned— one of the best. But, somehow, things went wrong. And the police there made the biggest bust they have ever made, supposedly with her help."

John listened intently, his focus unwavering.

"Well," …. Boran elaborated… "whether they made a bigger bust than this, no one knows. Over forty trucks, all full of people being smuggled from Asia, were intercepted and saved."

"We are talking about human trafficking, and it is not just any trafficking. This is a whole different scale," John said. His eyes narrowed as he glanced at Boran.

"When something like this is about to happen, it's not just anyone behind it. We are talking about someone who knows what they are doing." John added, deep in thought.

"Bingo," Boran replied, then with a mysterious look he asked him....

"Operations like this happen... when?"

"When everyone's distracted, and where everyone's looking the other way," John said, completing his thought.

"Exactly'.... Boran added.... "That's when **your** people," he said, pointing with his finger in quotation marks.... "Do the real work."

John stiffened, a dark look crossing his face.

"Don't know why, but everything in Manchester feels off," .... Boran continued.... "Is it just a coincidence that your friend's tangled up in this? And are we talking about the same person from five years ago" He added, making him think very seriously about what he had told him.

John paused, his mind racing.... "Interesting," he muttered.... "You're telling me she has been waiting five years to finish the job?"

"Or are we just calling this a coincidence?" Boran asked.

"Well, my uncle always said……There is no such thing as a coincidence. Nothing is random. Things happen when they are meant to. The rest of it is just decisions we must make after." John exclaimed.

Boran fell quiet, letting John's words take affect. "Wise words," he said.

John's study grew distant, as if seeing something that wasn't there.

"Yeah, wise guy," he muttered, remembering his uncle, the man who had always been so sure of his place in the world—before it eventually took him.

"My condolences," Boran said, quieter this time.

"No need," John responded…… "Let's move forward."

As they spoke, one of the officers discovered something worse: all the cameras had been turned off, and there was no evidence of the woman's presence. One officer stepped forward, his face tight. He called John out.

John stepped outside, nodding to the guards to hold tight, promising that they would continue with Boran tomorrow. The officer approached him with a grim look. "Nothing on the footage. The cameras were off. Nothings recorded."

John smirked darkly, under his breath. "Naturally, that's what I thought."

He scanned the room, sweeping over the faces of the people around him, his focus fixing on Sarah. There was something urgent in his eyes, something he did not want anyone else to see. As soon as he spotted her, he moved quickly, stepping away from the crowd, making his way toward her. He lowered his tone, making sure no one overheard.

"Sarah," he said.

She turned toward him, slightly surprised. "Yes, John? What's going on?"

He glanced around once more, ensuring they were alone, and then looked straight at her. "Can you do me a favour? Can you connect me with the chief of police in Manchester? It's important."

Sarah's confusion deepened...... "What? Why do you need to talk to them?"

He waited for a moment, his look intense. "Please, just do it, and don't tell anyone about this. Not a word."

Processing what he said she replied... "Why are you dragging me into this, John?"

He exhaled slowly, trying to lighten the mood... "Please, I promise this is the last time I'll ever ask you to make me coffee" ... he joked, a small attempt to ease the moment.

Sarah chuckled; it didn't take her long to agree...

"Fine. But don't make me regret this," she muttered, walking to her desk to get to work on his request.

At that time Maria, dressed in dark clothes and blending into the shadows, was crouched near Lee's apartment building. The evening sky was tinged with an orange glow from the setting sun, and the streets were quieter than usual, almost too quiet. She took a deep breath, scanning the area before moving forward.

Her fingers brushed the lock of the door, easing it open, a skill she had mastered over the years. As she stepped inside, the familiar smell of Lee's place greeted her — stale air mixed with a hint of fresh coffee. The lights were off, and the only sound was the soft hum of the city outside.

As Maria quietly moved deeper into the apartment, she heard a rustling sound. Turning, she saw John's cat — a familiar face from the past — walking toward her. The cat stopped in front of her, sniffing the air, before rubbing its head against her legs. Maria crouched down and ran her fingers through the cat's fur, her heart lifted with memories.

"You, John… you have changed. You've grown up… so much," she whispered, a soft smile tugging at her lips, though it didn't reach her eyes.

"I missed you… but wait a second. If you are here, then… Big John must be here too. He is living with you, watching over you, isn't he?"

Maria moved through the room, her hands skimming over objects, searching for something that would catch her attention. Somehow, she didn't see the pictures in the living room of John and Lee.

Back in the office, Sarah called John over with a slight nod of her head, her eyes sharp. John caught the look immediately. Without a word, he reached for the phone under his hand. The line hummed quietly, free for a moment, before someone on the other end picked up.

"Lieutenant Hannah speaking," came the voice. It was Hannah from Manchester—the woman who shared a bond with Maria that no one outside their circle fully understood.

"Good evening. Inspector John Wong here from the Miami Police Department," he replied, his purpose clear.

"Yes, how can I help you?" Hannah responded, a slight curiosity in her tone, though her professional façade remained unshaken.

Before John could speak further, the door to Hannah's office creaked open, and her secretary stepped inside with a message. Hannah, ever so subtle, gave a quiet signal to stay silent, her hand hovering in the air as she motioned for the secretary to wait.

"I'm calling, because I believe you might have information about a certain woman." John said with a little hope that maybe she can give him something about her.

There was a long pause on the line, their minds racing with questions. Hannah's voice came through again, this time more direct, tinged with both confusion and suspicion.

"What woman are you talking about?" she asked.

"She is about 170cm" … John continued… "With brown curly hair. And from what I saw, she is covered in tattoos—arms and back, too."

Hannah was silent for a moment…….. "Of course," … she finally replied, then she gently placed the receiver against her chest, letting out a long, drawn-out sigh.

"I knew it… I knew she would end up somewhere."

After a pause, she put the phone back to her ear, the silence growing.

"So, you know her," John said, his words calculated, eyes narrowing slightly. "I take it that's what your silence means?"

"Yes, Inspector," Hannah replied.

"Can I at least know what she's done?" .... There was a pause before she added, almost hesitantly, "She's not a bad person, but... can you at least tell me what she's gotten herself into?"

Her feelings, a mixture of protectiveness and worry slipping through the cracks in her usually composed demeanour.

"Actually, she hasn't done anything," John responded, though something seemed to linger behind his words. "She has even helped uncover a few things here, but I can't speak about them right now."

"Seriously?" Hannah's tone sharpened, her curiosity piqued.

"Yes," John replied.

"The reason I'm calling," he continued, "is that the case you had over a month ago... it could be connected to much more serious things happening here. And this woman... she's probably still involved in it. I think she knows things we clearly do not."

Hannah contemplated, though the sound was tinged with disbelief.

"Inspector, hold on. Maria is not a cop, or some secret agent. She is an incredibly good friend of mine—knows a lot, especially considering her background. She comes from a very wealthy family, and in her teenage years, she went through a lot with the wrong people. That's why she sometimes acts on instinct, having grown up in that kind of environment. I'm guessing she came to Miami to look for some clues about this guy named Franco."

"Yes, exactly," John said…… "But I can't give you any more details at this point."

"Hmm, I understand," Hannah replied. "Sounds like your boss doesn't know about this conversation."

"No, he doesn't," John said…. "I just wanted information about her."

"Her name is Maria Cafero," Hannah continued.

"You will not find anything on her in the system. As I said, she is not a criminal, and as I mentioned before, she comes from a wealthy background. I hope she stays out of trouble for your sake—when she sets her mind on something, she does it. Anyway, have a good evening."

"Same to you," John said. "Thanks for the intel."

"No problem," Hannah replied. "If I had not told you who she was, or if you had detained her, you would have figured it out eventually. But I did not do anything. Still, tell her to call me—I have not heard from her."

"Thanks again," John said, before hanging up the phone.

He sat back in his chair, a heavy sigh escaping him. "Well, that's strange," he muttered, the conversation settling in his mind. After hanging up the phone, Hannah turned to her secretary.

"What's so important?" she asked, her tone wrapped with curiosity. The secretary explained that Franco was indeed from Miami. Hannah nodded, her mind racing. She waved her off, allowing her to leave, then shut the door behind her.

Hannah could not shake the feeling of uncertainty. She stared at the empty room for a moment before muttering to herself, "Well, well… Let's see what you are going to do now, Maria." With that, she began gathering her things, preparing to leave, her mind still occupied with the strange turn of events.

At the same time, John was packing up, ready to head out as well. He had just parked his car along the street when something caught his attention—a man standing at the far side of the road, looking out of place. The scene felt unsettling, like an omen of something more to come. The man collapsed onto the pavement, John rushed over. Without waiting, he lifted him gently, checking to see if he was okay. The man was unresponsive, already unconscious. John carefully turned him onto his side, checking his pulse as he did so. He quickly reached into his bag, pulling out his trusty Nokia 2110, and dialled for an ambulance.

The paramedics arrived shortly, and John explained everything he had witnessed and the steps he had taken. They took the man away, and John, after ensuring everything was under control, turned to head home.

At the same time, Maria stood hidden on the terrace of John's apartment, silently watching the scene unfold. She did not realise the man helping was John, as she could not see either of their faces clearly. What struck her, though, was the act itself—the way people came together to help one another. She felt a quiet sense of comfort, a warm, reassuring feeling that humanity could still care for each other, even in the most unexpected situations.

As John entered his apartment, the cool air greeted him, his mind still lingering on the strange encounter in the street. He paused for a moment, standing still, as if trying to process the events.

The faint hum of the city outside filtered through the windows, a reminder that life was moving on, indifferent to the small dramas unfolding on its streets. His mind racing with thoughts about Maria and what might be happening next. He dropped his bag onto the couch, the load of the day still on his shoulders. He glanced around, searching for the familiar sound of his cat. "John, I'm home. Come on, it's time to eat," he called.

He placed his keys and gun on the dresser, flicked on the lights, and pulled off his t-shirt, making his way to the kitchen. The smell of something delicious hung in the air, and for a moment, he felt a fleeting sense of normalcy. But then, a strange tension gripped him as he realised, he was not alone.

Instinctively, he went back to the dresser, grabbed his gun, and moved cautiously toward the kitchen. His steps were quiet, deliberate. As he entered, the sight that met him was almost surreal— the table set with quality food, wine, and dancing candles. It was all too perfect, too calm, but there was no one there.

Just as he was about to turn back, he heard the soft sound of footsteps behind him. Maria appeared from the balcony, holding his cat in her arms, her eyes locking onto his with a mix of surprise and recognition. She paused for a heartbeat, just as he did. Neither of them had expected to see the other again so soon, and certainly not like this.

Maria's eyes widened, the realisation dawning on her as she looked at him, her lips curving into a wry smile. "Well, well," she said, her voice laced with disbelief, "So, we've met before... you're John, Lee's nephew." Her tone held a trace of amusement, of this strange twist of fate that had brought them back together.

John immediately, instinctively aimed his gun at her. His mind racing to catch up with the unexpected situation. He had not anticipated running into her again, and certainly not under these circumstances. "I guess we have," he replied, though his mind was still processing the strange sense of déjà vu.

"Drop him, now!" John commanded, pointing the gun at her with unblinking seriousness. "Alright, I'm letting him go," she said, releasing the cat to the ground. Maria wasn't fazed by the gun pointed at her. She remained nonchalantly calm. "I wouldn't hurt little John," she said, "but I never expected that today I'd meet big John…Drop the gun," she said nicely, "I'm not here to kill you… or something else……" her gaze flicking over his muscular frame with an almost casual interest. "I even made a meal, you know," she added with a slight smile, "but it's cold now. You took too long."

John's jaw tightened, his hand never wavering as the gun remained aimed at her, cold and serious. "Move" he ordered. His eyes did not leave hers, and without a word, they moved toward the living room.

Maria walked in first, but as soon as they were inside, she darted with quick precision. In an instant, she disarmed him, the gun now trained back on him, and she held it with effortless control. "You seem to have forgotten how easily I can take this from you," she said, her voice low, almost teasing.

John did not flinch. Within seconds, he grabbed the gun back from her, his body pressing against hers, cornering her against the wall. His chest was hard against her, and the barrel of the gun pressed just beneath her heart.

His voice was a low whisper against her ear. "You think you're the hero now?"

She met his gaze, unblinking, her eyes not portraying any fear.

"As I said, I'm not here to hurt you," she replied, her tone cool. "And I think it's a bit early for us to be this close, don't you think?"

The words hung there, charged with an electric pulse. For a moment, neither moved, both caught in the quiet wave of the encounter, where emotions ran just below the surface, threatening to break free.

John stepped back, his eyes still fixed on her, and then he spoke. "Alright then…Let's talk Maria." …he said.

She felt a brief surprise at hearing her name, her eyebrow slightly raised.

"So, you asked around about me," she said with a flicker of irony.

"But this isn't enough," John replied challenging, before he walked off to his room. He returned moments later, casually slipping on a t-shirt, his movements deliberate. "Let's get to know each other then," he said, his tone quieter now, but no less serious. "Seems we have something in common.

He settled on the couch, leaning forward, eyes still locked on hers. "How do you know my uncle?"

Maria's expression shifted, her thoughts racing for a moment before she answered.

"I'm sorry about your uncle," she said softly. "We were old friends… He helped me through some difficult times."

John's eyes did not soften.

"How did he die?" The question was sharp and direct to him.

"He… he killed himself," John said, his face unreadable. "He was fired. He could not handle it."

Maria recoiled as if she had been struck. "What?" she whispered, shock and anger mixing in her actions. "That doesn't make sense." She began pacing, her mind refusing to settle on the reality of what he had just told her. "No. That's impossible."

She stopped suddenly, her brow hardening as she turned to face him.

"He would never have done that. Not him." Her voice shook with disbelief, taking a step forward, trying to understand.

"Lee was—he was a man who valued things that went beyond material. The spiritual, the deeper meaning of life. It was not about the job, about the money. That was not who he was. He would never have taken his own life just because they fired him. Not him."

Maria's words were a mixture of grief and confusion, the very idea of Lee succumbing to something so horrid against everything she had ever known about him. To her, Lee was always the one who saw beyond the surface of life, a man who stood firm in his beliefs, never letting something as trivial as a job or money break him. That is why this news felt like a betrayal, something her mind could not reconcile.

The silence between them was firm, the only sound was little John eating food. John's eyes never left Maria as he spoke.

"I think the same," he admitted. "But I can't prove it. All the evidence leads to suicide."

Maria's gaze sharpened, her mind working. She was not about to let it go.

"That does not sit right……. "Something's wrong here." She tilted her head slightly, studying him. "What was he working on?"

John exhaled, frustration lining his features. "I don't know. He was secretive. Never said a thing. But not because he was afraid. He was calm—too calm." His eyes darkened as the words pressed down on him.

Maria absorbed this, the gears in her mind clicking into place. She paced, her steps measured, precise. "He must've known something," she murmured, almost to herself.

"Something he was not supposed to. And whatever it was, it cost him his life." She stopped abruptly and turned to face him. "And if they fired him, someone had to have a reason… someone in your circle."

John's eyes showed a hint of uncertainty, but he kept composure.

"But I've checked everyone. No one has anything to hide. They are clean. Nothing to pin on anyone. Even if it's true…" He said.

Maria's hand froze, her fingers brushing the surface of a small object she had almost forgotten about. The realisation hit her hard.

"The secret room!" she exclaimed, urgent. Without waiting, she moved swiftly toward the living room, her pace quickening.

"A secret room?" John was hit with disbelief, but he followed her, his eyes glued to her every movement.

She did not answer, her focus locked on the wall in front of her. There, hidden within the seams of the furniture, was a small compartment. Her fingers slid into the gap, finding the familiar shape she had been searching for. Slowly, methodically, she pulled out a small, worn keychain—something John's uncle had left behind, something she knew would be important.

"Did your uncle leave you something like this?" she asked, holding it out to him, her eyes searching his face for any sign of recognition.

John watched the keychain in her hand. "Yeah. That's—wait." He stepped forward, a frown creeping in as she pulled it away from him. "What is that?" He questioned.

Before he could finish, Maria had already twisted the keychain, unlocking a hidden mechanism in the wall. A key slipped out into her palm, its metal cool against her skin. Without another word, she strode toward the door, the thoughts of what lay ahead pressing on her.

John's confusion shifted to curiosity as he watched her approach the locked door. Maria did not hesitate—she unlocked it with ease, pushing the door open to reveal a small room, cluttered with her personal items, books, and remnants of a life she thought she had buried. She stepped inside, the atmosphere in the room felt dense, filled with the memories of a time long passed. Her eyes moved over the familiar clutter—things that reminded her of days spent in this very room. John lingered at the threshold, his gaze sweeping over the room. He entered; his presence was a silent demand for answers. Maria stood motionless for a moment, her fingers brushing against the books on the shelf, feeling the past swirl around her like a storm. "This," she whispered, her voice barely audible, "this is where it all began."

A flash of memories washed over her mind…… The room was bathed in soft, golden light, a mix of sunlight and the gentle tap of rain against the window. Maria lay on the bed, her face buried in her hands, her body trembling as she quietly sobbed. The memories of this room took her back to a painful place.

Lee stood nearby, his voice calm, a steady anchor in the midst of her storm. "Maria, I've lit a candle for you. There's warm tea waiting. Everything is going to be okay."

Her breath caught in her throat; she did not look up immediately. Lee did not rush her, just stayed quiet, waiting for her to gather herself. After a long moment, she lifted her head, the tears still fresh on her cheeks. She felt the warmth of the space, and yet, her mind was still a blizzard.

Lee crouched next to her, his presence calm and grounded. "Take a deep breath. Let your mind settle. A peaceful mind always finds the answers."

His words echoed in her mind, and the memory of them flooded her senses.

"A peaceful mind always finds the answers." The mantra she had long forgotten, now coming back with clarity in the quiet of the room. She repeated it silently to herself, letting the words take hold. She closed her eyes, trying to calm the racing thoughts.

John looked at her, a confused expression crossing his face.

"What? What are you talking about?" he asked. "How come I didn't know about this room?" Maria quickly snapped back to reality, the memory fading almost as soon as it arrived.

"I lived here," she replied, though something unspoken lingered between them.

She turned to him, her eyes sharp with purpose. "Let's search for something," she said, though she was not sure exactly what they were looking for, but the instinct was strong. "Search for what?" he asked, curiosity knitting his brow.

"This room, it was mine," she continued, almost as if speaking to herself. "Yes," she confirmed when he pressed further. "I told you; Uncle Lee helped me through difficult times. Really hard times."

John nodded slowly, absorbing her words. "I get that," he said, a hint of skepticism in his tone. "But why the secrecy? And why did he help you when you have everything—money, wealth? Or maybe your teenage years were… a little wild?" he suggested, searching for answers.

Maria paused, she looked at him, directly.

"I see. You spoke with Hannah, didn't you?" she said, suddenly understanding.

"Well, I had to ask around, here and there," John admitted, almost apologetic. "I needed the information."

Maria shook her head, but there was something about the words John had spoken that piqued her curiosity. Then, her attention was caught.

"What's this?" John asked, pointing to a note pinned on the wall. He handed it to her, his eyes flaring with suspicion.

She read the note aloud, her voice barely above a whisper. "Death is only the beginning"

A chill ran through her, her mind racing to understand. "Huh… strange," she murmured, her eyes lingering on the note.

"What does this mean? Does it mean he knew something? So strange." John said.

They both stood there, staring at the cryptic message, a sense of unease settling between them. The room, once familiar, now felt cold and distant, as if the walls themselves were holding secrets, and the note was just the beginning.

"I don't know, I'm not sure," she added, "but we'll find out." She paused for a moment, then said, "I should go."

"Whoever asks you for something, no matter what the information is, don't tell anyone until we know who to trust and who not to," she warned him.

"Do you have anywhere to go?" he asked.

"You can stay here, in the room that was meant for you," he added.

She turned to look at him, lost in thought for a moment, then said, "That's very kind. Maybe I'm starting to like you."

John laughed and said, "Don't get ahead of yourself, it's only our first meeting. I still have not figured you out. By the way, I'm the prankster here, do not try to copy me."

They both laughed.

"Alright, what are you saying?" Maria responded. "Come on, John," she said to the cat, picking it up. "Let's leave big John to sleep alone. Good night."

Chapter 5

$\mathcal{A}$ few days later, in the apartment, John kept Maria hidden while she went through the cases Lee had worked on, trying to uncover more about his suicide.

One early morning, they sat in the car, watching the building across the street and listened to some music. Maria leaned in and asked John what they were doing here. He explained that they were waiting for the lover of Boran, the Albanian man from the club they had caught. She lived across the street, and since John had been taking care of his family's safety for a while, they were now just waiting to see if someone it's going to check the apartment.

Soon enough, two cars pulled up across the street, parking with a soft screech of tires. A few men got out of the cars and headed toward the building. Maria and John, noticing them, immediately followed, blending into the crowd, careful not to draw attention. The street was alive, full of people bustling about, unaware of the quiet tension unfolding.

One of the men unlocked the door and they entered the apartment, their movements swift and precise. They searched the rooms with quiet urgency but found no one inside. Their disappointment was short-lived as they began to search more thoroughly, scanning for anything of interest.

Just then, a muffled noise from the corridor caught their attention. They quickly retreated behind the kitchen wall, holding their breath. The sound of footsteps grew louder. The door creaked open, followed by the unmistakable meow of a cat and a woman's voice calling out sweetly, "Oh, kitty, my sweet little one, I almost forgot to get you food."

The men exchanged confused glances. A cat? They had not noticed anything about a pet here. They waited in silence as the door clicked shut again, the woman's voice trailing off as she mentioned she would grab food for the cat.

Once the door was firmly closed, they let out a collective sigh.

They stepped out from behind the wall, ready to move. That's when they saw Maria and John standing by the door, waiting for them. She smiled gently, her presence steady and intense.

"I'm so sorry," she said. "I don't have a cat here, actually... I do have one, but in another home."

Before the men could react, John moved into position beside Maria. Time seemed to slow down, just as quickly as the confusion had settled, the fighting began. The men lunged forward, but Maria and John were ready. They moved fluidly, their trained bodies reacting with precision. They knew their way around a fight, each blow executed with purpose, their movements coordinated, as if they had done this a thousand times before.

The men were skilled, but Maria and John were just as formidable, their martial arts flowing like a dance. The fight was intense, but the outcome was inevitable—the thugs were quickly overpowered.

As the men lay on the ground, John took a deep breath, glancing at Maria with a mix of exhaustion and admiration. "I didn't know you knew kung fu," he said, still catching his breath.

Maria looked back at him with a small, amused smile. "Same with you but you're pretty good," she replied, her tone light, yet a hint of respect in her eyes.

"Well, even though I'm all blonde and handsome like my mom, I'm still half-Chinese, you know? Do not forget that" John said, laughing lightly.

Maria shot him a glance and smiled but didn't say anything. Then, the sound of a phone ringing broke the moment. It was coming from the jacket of the main bruiser, vibrating urgently. Maria quickly went over, grabbed the phone, and answered it. A voice on the other end spoke rapidly in Portuguese.

"You're taking too long, what's going on?" the voice demanded.

Maria glanced at John, knowing he was half-Brazilian and spoke Portuguese. John took the phone from her and, without missing a beat, responded fluently.

"They will be a little bit late. Because I'm going to take them to the police station"

Before the conversation could continue, the line went dead, cutting off abruptly.

"Portuguese?" Maria wondered to herself. This can't be, she murmured quietly.

"What? Why are you so surprised?" John teased her.

"I think that voice sounds familiar, and if I'm right, I think I know who's behind your uncle's murder," Maria said, profoundly serious.

"What?" John looked at her, shocked and confused.

"Yes," Maria replied. "Now, signal the police, get these people out of here, and then, after lunch, meet me at the café where Lee used to go."

John stared at her, still confused, pretending not to understand. She continued, "You should know it anyway… It's a little retro café, a perfect place for nice meetings. Remember?"

"Yes, I think I remember. Wait, are you inviting me on a date now?" John added with a playful grin.

"Oh, you wish, huh?" Maria laughed and looked at him again, teasing.

John laughed too, unable to hold it in.

"And one more thing," Maria said. "Try to get some information on Samara Cabal."

And with that she left.

At the police station, John was digging through files, trying to gather more information about Samara Cabal. It did not take long for him to realise that her case was the last one his uncle, Lee, had worked on. He immediately asked Sarah to dig up and provide all the information they had on her.

Meanwhile, Maria was in John's apartment. She lit a few candles around the bathtub, focusing on her chakras, and placed precious stones all around. The soft glow of the candles filled the bathroom, creating a serene atmosphere. She filled the bathtub with warm water, undressed, and stepped in, letting the soothing heat envelop her as she sank into the water, her mind drifting away.

Maria submerged herself deeply in the bath once more, then resurfaced and closed her eyes tightly. The warm water embraced her. Memories began to flood in, vivid and sharp, the sounds and sights as if they had happened just moments ago.

She found herself back in an apartment. The sunlight streamed in through the large windows, casting an amazing ray across the room. The apartment was beautiful and elegant, with a sense of peace, but that serenity was shattered by the tension between her and Samara. The sleek furniture, the gentle hum of life outside, all felt distant now, as if it were part of another world. Samara was there, standing tall by her desk, her sharp gaze focused on Maria, full of superiority and coldness. Guard stood behind her, their weapons aimed in her direction, but Maria didn't flinch.

"This isn't the solution," Maria had said, trying to remain calm, despite the danger pressing in on her.

Samara, with all her arrogance, barely moved. She looked down at Maria, as if she were an insect beneath her boot.

"On the contrary," Samara had replied, her eyes narrowing with disdain.

"Ever since you entered our lives, you have been trying to destroy everything. Your so-called virtue, your idealism… it's all a lie. You can either lead or you are nothing but a pawn. You are just… unnecessary." She added.

Maria had struggled to keep her composure, the weight of Samara's words digging in. She had spent so much of her life fighting for good, for right, for justice, but Samara was right about one thing—this world did not always care for those ideals.

"You think you're a leader?" Maria asked, her heart pounding in her chest.

Samara sneered, her stance unwavering… "Of course, I am. Something you could never be……. You are pathetic, and I won't allow my son to turn out like you. Look at you—weak, always playing the victim. I'm not like you. I'll make sure he's strong, powerful. He will never be as helpless as you."

Maria swallowed the bitterness rising in her throat.

"But he doesn't want to be like you," she countered. "You have already twisted him into something he is not. What kind of mother pushes her son into a world of crime and corruption?"

Samara's expression hardened, her eyes turning to steel as she stood up from her desk, towering over Maria. "I'm the kind of mother who does whatever it takes to make her son powerful. I want him to be untouchable. Nothing and no one should break him. And everything I do, every decision, is for his good. To make sure he is never weak like you, never pathetic."

Maria looked at her, her heart heavy with pity. "So, you will take away his humanity, then? You will strip him of everything that makes him decent just to make him strong in your eyes?"

Samara let out a cold laugh, one that rang through the room like a bell of finality. "Humanity? You are still thinking in those terms?" she scoffed, her voice laced with contempt. "Don't be foolish. There is no place for that anymore. Not in this world. Either you rule, or you are ruled. There is no middle ground, no room for softness. As I said, either you are a king, a queen, or you are just a pawn, pushed in every way where they're told to be"

Maria stood on the chair, feeling the adrenaline surge through her veins. In one swift motion, she kicked the knee of the guard holding a gun towards her. He fell to the floor, and without hesitation, she stepped on him, hitting him with her elbow across his face. The gun was now in her hands, and she pointed it directly at Samara, who remained seated, unshaken, as though completely unbothered by the threat.

"Look at you!" Samara said, her eyes full of scorn, as if she were staring at something beneath her. "What?" she continued with arrogance. "Are you really going to use violence, or are you just pretending that you're a threat?"

She leaned back in her chair, seemingly at ease, a smirk playing on her lips.

"You can't hurt me," Samara said confidently. "Because, let me think… Oh, yes, everyone can be the best version of themselves if they want to be."

She laughed, the sound sharp and dismissive. "Sweetheart, I'm already in my best version, and everyone sees it."

Her words, delivered with such pride, as though she never questioned her own power, as if she were invincible in her own eyes.

Maria hesitated for a moment, keeping her gun aimed at Samara, and said:

"Everyone sees what they want to see, but not everyone stands behind their decisions justly, because the choices you make in life shape the person you become."

"You're right, I can't hurt you" Maria continued, lowering the gun and starting to disassemble it. Samara laughed at this.

"But do you know why?" Maria asked. "Because you're already hurt enough as you are."

Samara stood still, her expression hardening, her gaze filled with anger as she glared at Maria.

"You're so hurt," Maria went on with bitterness… "that you cannot even find joy in the simple things. You are so blinded by power, money, the need to control, and always be above others, that nothing else matters to you. Everyone else is just an animal beneath your feet. What matters is your ego. What matters is being number one."

Samara stood tall, her chest swelling with pride as she met Maria's survey. "Yes," she said firmly, "I am number one. And I will continue to be number one."

"And what exactly are you number one at?" Maria's eyes locked deeply onto Samara's, her question cutting through the tense air. But instead of waiting for an answer, she turned toward the window. The sunlight poured in, casting a glow across her face. Maria stared at the sky for a few seconds, lost in thought. Then, as if gathering her resolve, she turned back toward Samara, stepping slightly away.

"And how long will you remain number one?" She was calm, every word carrying meaning. "Everything is temporary," Maria continued. "Your power is temporary. Your money, your manipulations, your ego — all temporary."

She glanced around, gesturing at the luxurious apartment that reflected nothing but wealth. The sunlight bounced off the polished surfaces, making the room feel even grander. But Maria's gaze returned to Samara, piercing through the façade.

"One day — maybe tomorrow, maybe the next — you'll lie in a bed, weak and helpless," Maria said, continuing…. "And when you leave this world, you will not take a shred of it with you. Not your ego, not your pride, not your power. You will leave just as you came — with nothing."

Samara's face remained rigid, but a flicker of anger in her eyes betrayed her. She slowly reached for the telephone on her desk, her fingers curling around the receiver. Without breaking eye contact from Maria, she dialled a number and spoke in Portuguese, with a commanding demeanour.

"Antonio, come to my office immediately, and take care of this… guest who is overstayed her welcome."

"Right away, ma'am," came the voice on the other end. "But we have a slight problem."

"A problem?" Samara's jaw tightened. "What kind of problem?"

"Your son is here, ma'am. He is with a police officer. They are already on their way to your office."

"What?" A violence in Samara's voice, "And you're telling me this now?"

"I tried to stop them, ma'am, but I couldn't." Antonio replied.

Maria's breath was steady, the water still around her. Yet the echoes of the past lingered in her mind. The strong sunlight from the memory seemed to fade, replaced by the dim glow of the candles. The warmth of the bathwater barely reached her as she opened her eyes. Droplets ran down her skin, but the pounding in her head was all she could feel.

It struck her then. The voice. The memory had brought it back with a clarity she could not ignore. The man on the phone, the one in the apartment - it was him. Antonio. Samara's right hand. The realisation twisted in her stomach.

Maria stood up, droplets of water tracing down her skin, the balmy air from the bathroom brushing against her. The memory still echoed in her mind - Samara's cutting words, the weight of her own choices, but there was no time to waste. She pulled on her bathrobe, her hands trembling slightly, though she would not allow herself to acknowledge it. The bathroom mirror reflected her face, but it was more than just a reflection. It was a reminder.

The door closed softly behind her as she left the apartment. Outside, the world moved on, oblivious to the tidal wave inside her. The city's sounds drowned her steps, but her thoughts were screaming on one thing — John.

Meanwhile, the café pulsed with a quiet rhythm. The soft clink of coffee cups and murmured conversations mixed with the low hum of an old ceiling fan. It was the kind of place that held stories — fleeting moments of strangers' lives intertwining. But today, Maria's presence carried a pain that none of the other patrons could see.

John sat near the window, his laptop glowing in front of him, the screen's reflection displaying in his eyes. Papers were scattered across the table, and a half-empty cup of coffee sat beside him. His fingers tapped restlessly against the table, but his mind was somewhere far beyond the walls of the café.

When Maria stepped inside, she didn't pause. There was no hesitation. Her gaze locked onto him, and the smell of the café dimmed in her mind. For a brief moment, the warmth of the sunlight touched her face, almost like a reminder that there was still light — even now.

John didn't notice her at first, the tenseness of his shoulders betraying the thoughts he carried. As Maria drew closer, the presence of her shadow falling across the table made him look up. Their eyes met.

"It's time," John said.

"I'm sorry," Maria replied, sitting beside him.

"Well, what is the news? Did you find anything?" she asked.

"Actually, look," John said, showing her the laptop with all the information about Samara Cabal.

"Five years ago," he continued, "my uncle got her locked up in Miami prison."

In that moment, Maria drifted for a second, remembering how she and his Uncle Lee had sat at the opposite table in this very café, having a serious conversation.

"Good job, Lee," she said. "Good thing you caught her, or she would've escaped."

"It wasn't hard to catch her," Lee replied.

"The hard part was how to keep her locked up. But with all the evidence you gave me, she can't move from that prison now."

Maria sighed for a moment and then looked at him.

"Maybe she'll change," she said softly. "I really hope she does."

Lee looked at her with a knowingly.

"People like her don't change," he said. "When you cannot find peace within yourself, chaos swallows you whole and starts to control you. I'm not saying it is impossible to find your way back to yourself— actually, it's not that hard—but the fear that chaos inside you gives you makes you think there is no way out, and that you must be what you are." he added.

Maria looked at him, almost as if to herself, said, "But hope dies last, right? Maybe she can change."

Lee chuckled softly.

"You see," he continued, "even after losing your loved ones, you still see hope and goodness in people. That is what makes you special. You do not let chaos control you. You control it."

Maria's thoughts lingered in that moment, but then, she snapped back to the present as John waved his hand in front of her face.

"Hey, hey!" he said softly. "Where did you go? I'm talking to you."

"Sorry," she whispered, shaking off the memory. "I just… got lost in thought for a second. So many memories here with your uncle, Lee."

"I know," John replied softly "I have my own memories with him too."

But his words brought her back, gently steering her to reality.

"Let's focus on what's in front of us right now," he said.

"Wait a second," Maria's eyes drifted back to the laptop. "It says here that Uncle Lee worked on her case again."

"Yeah, actually, it was his last case," John confirmed.

"A year and a half ago, the prison where Samara Cabal was held caught fire, and she died in it."

"Interesting…, You're saying she's dead?" Maria quizzed.

"Yeah, this is her death certificate," John said.

"I don't think she's dead," Maria replied.

"My uncle didn't believe it either and tried to prove it." John noted.

Maria and John continued their conversation at the café, weighing every possible scenario, every angle.

At the same time, in the police station, Sarah was dialling her phone, her hand shaking slightly as anxiety crept in.

"Come on, come on, pick up," she muttered under her breath, her voice tight with urgency. She could feel time quickly moving on.

And then, finally, the line clicked, and it was her—Samara Cabal. She was lounging by her pool somewhere in Miami, completely unaware of the mess brewing. The servants handed her the phone, and she answered, her voice cool but distant.

"Hello?" Samara said, clearly not expecting anything unusual.

"Ma'am," Sarah's tone was strained, urgent. "Listen to me, it's Sarah…. You need to evacuate, immediately. Your identity… that you are still alive… it is about to be exposed."

"What?!" Samara's voice cracked with disbelief. She jumped to her feet, panic rising.

"What are you saying? This is impossible!" Samara replied with anger.

"Lee's nephew," Sarah pressed on…. "He has ordered the funeral home to dig up your body and run another test; to prove it's really you. I've tried everything, tried to stop him… but I could not. It's too late."

Samara's breath caught in her throat. "How could this happen?" she demanded.

"It's because of something his uncle Lee left him behind…...Before he died, your case was his last… and now, it's all unraveling." Sarah said, as if fearfully hoping to not anger.

Samara's hand tightened around the phone, her face a mask of fury and fear. "That damn Lee," she hissed under her breath, the words dripping with venom. "Even from the grave, he won't let me be."

Then Samara continued, "Well, what else? Is there anything else besides that?"

"Anything else?" Sarah wondered. "Ah, actually, yes," Sarah remembered.

"There is, madam. Someone is helping John. A woman named Maria. I've looked into her. She comes from a very wealthy background, from England. And the other thing is…"

"The other thing is what?" Samara pressed with growing restlessness.

"Madam, your failure in Manchester… it's because of her," Sarah replied, her tone measured but urgent.

"What?" Samara was taken aback. "How could some rich girl get involved in something like this? How can she be behind such a massive operation?"

"I looked into it," Sarah said. "Our associates in Manchester told me she had connections… with a lot of people. Law enforcement too, but I couldn't dig up anything more. She is just a connector, it seems. A player in the shadows."

"Ahaa… the rats," Samara muttered under her breath, her anger simmering beneath the surface. She lowered the phone, letting a string of curses slip from her lips in Portuguese, then pressed the phone back to her ear with a sharp exhale.

"Listen to me carefully," Samara said, a serious tone in her voice.

"I have got a few big moves to make here. If I pass through Brazil, you'd better keep me in the loop, and I will take over from there."

"Alright, madam," Sarah replied, tension creeping in. She hung up, the strain of their conversation lingering.

At that moment, in the café, Maria and John were still deep in conversation. Maria, her fingers absently tracing the edge of the coffee cup, suddenly furrowed her brow. She had been thinking about everything for a while, the pieces of the puzzle finally clicking together. "Of course," she murmured to herself, "how didn't I see it? Human trafficking…" Her thoughts darkened, but she quickly turned to John.

"Did you manage to get them to do a new test on her body?" she asked.

John shifted in his seat, clearly uneasy. He glanced at her before responding, his words coming out a little too quickly. "Yeah, I have already contacted the agency. We're trying to get the body out… and have it tested. We should have the results in a couple of days."

Maria studied him, her look sharp. "A couple of days?" She leaned forward slightly…... "You think it will take that long? If she really is alive—and I have every reason to believe she is— by then, she will be long gone. She will have vanished, and we will not be able to find her."

John's hands tightened around his cup, his eyes darting around the café. There was something on his mind, something he was not saying.

"You think she'll find out we're doing a new test on her body?" he asked, betraying a hint of unease.

Maria's lips tightened into a thin line. "If she doesn't already know…" she said quietly.

Maria looked at the folder besides John's laptop, her gaze intense as she locked eyes with him.

"Who gave you this folder?" she asked sharply.

"Sarah!" John replied with a little pride in his eyes … "She's a very good colleague and a friend."

Maria stood up suddenly, her face hardening. "John! There's wrong information in this folder. It says that after Samara Cabal's death, no one bothered to prove it was not her and that the case was closed when she was declared dead. But on Lee's laptop, it says he tried to follow up, to prove it really was her, and that the Samara Cabal case was his last."

"How long have you known this…… Sarah?" Maria asked, intensely.

"What?" John laughed nervously. "No, there is no way. Sarah's a good person. She has been great with everything. Actually, she's been helping me from the very beginning, since I arrived." He let out a hollow laugh, then added, "Yeah, she's been helping me constantly."

He stared at Maria, a sudden realisation hitting him.

"How did I not see this!" He slammed his hand on the table, cursing under his breath.

"Hey, it's okay!" Maria said, sitting back down across from him. "You know, sometimes it's okay to not be okay. So don't regret it. Don't regret learning things this way, but hey, everyone has their story. Let us hear hers, huh?"

"You know what?" Maria continued, shifting with a new thought. "I have an idea…"

Chapter 6

At the same time, Samara was walking through her lavish house, giving orders to have everything packed and ready for the journey ahead. After a while, her right hand, Antonio, entered the room. They exchanged a few words in Portuguese.

"Madam," he asked, "What's going on? Are we leaving for somewhere?"

"Antonio," she turned to him, eyes narrowing. "Where have you been all day? I sent you to take care of a simple task, and you have been missing for hours."

"I know, madam," he replied, apologetically…. "Forgive me, I was delayed. There were… complications."

"Complications?" Samara asked coldly, stepping closer to him. She leaned in, whispering in his ear. "Antonio, do you know why you're my right hand?"

"Yes, madam," he answered, his voice direct. "Because I don't allow complications."

She studied him for a long moment, her eyes lighting with fire, before stepping back slightly. "You know what happened to Franco, don't you?"

"Yes, madam, I know," he replied, the prominence of her words sinking in.

"He also didn't allow complications, did he?" she continued, … "And when he couldn't handle it anymore, he took the easy way out. He chose to end his life because he knew what would be waiting for him if he stayed alive."

Antonio stood frozen, the pressure between them rising.

"Madam," he finally said, his voice filled with understanding, "I completely grasp your point. Forgive me."

"So, then what's the problem?" she pressed, her posture straightening.

"The problem is Lee's nephew," Antonio answered, a frustration showing from his eyes. "He's got our men—those who went after the Albanian's girl." He added.

Samara exhaled deeply, her face hardening as she looked at him once more.

"You know," she said, a slight smile creeping onto her lips, "today is going to be a very good day."

She glanced at him with a sly look. "You were asking what is going on here, weren't you? Well, Antonio, we are heading back to Brazil. I think it's about time. As they say, every storm eventually passes, and the stone always finds its place. I have been missing our homeland, so get ready. We have got to act fast, because Lee's nephew is on the verge of proving I'm not dead."

In the warm glow of the early evening, John and Sarah sat across from each other in an elegant restaurant, the soft clinking of glasses and hushed conversations surrounding them.

Sarah's heart raced with excitement; she had admired John for so long.

"John, what made you invite me out tonight?" she asked him, the excitement showing on her face.

John smiled, his gaze steady. "You have always been my rock, Sarah. From the very beginning, you have been there for me. Inviting you out—it's the least I can do after everything you have done."

Sarah's eyes softened. "That's so sweet of you."

He shook his head gently. "No, you're the sweet one here."

As they continued their conversation, the atmosphere around them seemed to shift, growing more intimate.

Sarah's eyes sparkled with curiosity. "So, what's next for us, John? What is our next adventure?"

John leaned in and said…. "I believe it's about cherishing these moments together, discovering what truly makes us happy. Whether it's facing challenges or just enjoying simple joys, we will do it together."

Sarah's heart swelled with emotion, and she reached across the table, taking his hand in hers. "Together, then," she whispered, a smile spreading across her face.

Just as the conversation between John and Sarah flowed, the waiter approached, his presence momentarily pulling them from their quiet moment.

"Are you ready to order?" he asked politely.

"Yes," Sarah replied with a nice look to the waiter…… "I'll have the caprese salad and a glass of Prosecco, please."

"Of course," the waiter nodded, then turned to John. "And for you, sir?"

"I'm not really hungry," John said, casual yet thoughtful, "but let's go with a bottle of Prosecco and two glasses."

The waiter acknowledged the order and disappeared into the distance.

John leaned back slightly, getting comfortable.

"Tonight," he said softly, his look carrying some anticipation, "let's just unwind a little, forget the world." Sarah's eyes brightened immediately, her lips curving into a smile, and the conversation between them deepened, more relaxed now.

As they spoke, far from the restaurant's cozy atmosphere, Samara was already in her private jet, heading back to Brazil. She sat in the plush seats, sipping from her glass of champagne, her eyes coldly fixed ahead. Taking a serious phone call, in rapid Portuguese.

"I told you something came up, do I need to tell you what? All you need to know is I'm coming back. Do I need to explain more?" Samara's voice was tense. "Instead of being glad your mother's coming home, you're upset with me!"

Gabriel, Samara's son, was at his house in Rio, listening to her strained words. He couldn't figure out why she was returning so suddenly.

"No, mom!" he said, frustrated. "Of course, I'll be happy to see you, but why now?"

"I'll explain when I get there," Samara replied. "How's everything with you?"

"Everything's fine," Gabriel answered. "Business is good, the drugs sell easily, like always."

"Good. I will see you soon," Samara said before hanging up.

Gabriel sat back, the conversation still bothering him. His thoughts were interrupted as Lilly, his American girlfriend from Miami, entered the room. She was beautiful, but there was something colder beneath her polished exterior.

"What's up, baby? You look stressed," Lilly said, noticing his mood.

"Nothing," Gabriel replied. "Just get ready for tonight, we have guests."

Lilly raised an eyebrow with surprise. "Guests...... Is it important?"

"No, it's not a business thing," … Gabriel said… "My mom's coming."

Lilly smiled, but it was tight.

"Well, try to be nice," he said, his tone dripping with sarcasm. "Don't let her see your true self."

As Gabriel walked out, Lilly's eyes followed him. With a smirk, she muttered to herself, "Why is that old witch coming now to ruin everything?"

And so, everyone began preparing in the house for Samara's arrival. Meanwhile, in Miami, the evening continued, and John took Sarah to her apartment. Just before leaving, standing at her door, he said, "Hey, it was nice to spend time with you!"

"Yeah, it was great!" she replied, smiling.

"Then I will leave you here. We will see each other tomorrow at work, right?"

"If you want, come in for a bit," she suggested.

"No, I can't," he replied. "I have got a lot of work. From what I learned, this Samara is from Brazil, and I suspect we have someone in the administration reporting to her. I need to find out what is really going on."

"Really?" she asked, worried at first, but then she calmed herself down, not wanting to draw attention.

"Do you think this woman has someone in our administration?"

"Yes," he answered. "But I don't know who, and it could be anyone."

"Anyone, like me?" she joked.

"YOU?" John asked, pretending to be shocked. "Why you? You are my most trusted person; it can't be you," he added.

"I was just kidding," she said. "Of course, I wouldn't do something like that. Now go, get some sleep. We will see each other tomorrow."

"Alright," John said. "You go rest too. Good night," and he kissed her on the cheek.

"Good night, John," she whispered, then returned to her apartment, feeling uneasy.

She began talking to herself. "It's impossible, how and where does he know so much?" Anxiously, she paced around her living room, put on her robe, lit a cigarette, and dialled Mrs. Cabal's number from her landline.

"Come on, please, pick up," she muttered to herself, but the line just rang, and eventually, it went to voicemail. Of course, Sarah left a message.

"Mrs. Cabal," she began, little worried…... "John, Lee's nephew, knows you are alive for sure. He even knows you are returning to Brazil, and what is worse, he suspects someone in the administration is reporting everything to you. He is about to expose it. If I'm not careful, things could get out of hand. For now, everything is under control. He trusts me a lot, but I need to cover for you to keep you safe."

After hanging up the phone and barely catching her breath, John stepped out from the hallway into the living room. The moment Sarah saw him, her face went pale, her body stiffening as fear gripped her.

"This… this is exactly what I never expected from you, Sarah," he said, with great disappointment in his face.

"You…" Her words faltered, shock evident in her eyes. "But how did you get in? What are you doing here?"

Maria emerged beside him, calm yet unwavering…... "I let him in. I have been in the apartment all afternoon, searching for evidence."

Sarah's focus snapped to her, confusion flashing before the realisation struck.

"You… wait. You are that Maria, aren't you? Shameless Maria! How dare you!" She said with anger as she lunged forward, but John quickly stepped in, holding her back.

"Stop!" His voice cutting through the tension, sharp and commanding.

"After all these years… I can't believe it." His eyes locked onto hers, pain ridden.

"No, John! You don't understand!" Sarah's voice trembled, her hands shaking. Then, turning her fury toward Maria, she spat out.

"It's all your fault!" She moved to strike, but John intercepted her once more, his presence unyielding.

"Her fault?" getting confused, each word heavy with emotion.

"And why would it be her fault, Sarah? Is she the one who chose to hide behind lies, pretending to be someone she is not? Is she the one who twisted the truth and betrayed the people who trusted her? Is she the reason you are standing here like this?"

He shook his head, his disappointment sinking into every word. "No. That was you…. And yet, somehow, it's easier for you to point your finger at someone else. Pretend you are blameless. As if your choices did not bring you to this moment."

The silence that followed was deafening. John's tone softened, but the pain remained.

"And I thought you were better than this, Sarah. I thought you were a strong, honourable officer. But maybe I was wrong."

John, you don't get it!" Sarah tried to explain. She motioned around the apartment, her frustration spilling over.

"Do you see all of this?" she asked, her gestures emphasising the luxurious space.

"Tell me, John, how could I afford all this on my miserable salary? Wanting a better life — is that really a crime?"

John looked around, filled with disbelief…. "Do you even hear yourself, Sarah? A better life, at the cost of others' suffering? At the expense of the innocent people, which you are supposed to protect every single day. Is that the life you are proud of?"

"Stop!" she shot back, her face twisting in anger. "You really don't get it…You are just accusing me! What have I done that is so unforgivable?"

John's expression hardened, the confrontation pressing down on him.

"You're either above them all or buried beneath them," she said coldly. Her indifference gnawed at him. He searched her eyes, desperate for even a shade of regret.

"What? Are you serious? You really don't feel even a shred of guilt for what you have done?" He asked her.

Before he could continue, Maria stepped forward. "John, stop," she said softly……

"There's no point." Maria added.

Just then, the door burst open. Police officers entered the apartment, their presence filling the room with undeniable finality. Without a word, they approached Sarah, preparing to arrest her. But even as the handcuffs clicked around her wrists, she twisted back toward Maria, her glare sharp and bitter. "This is your fault!" she cursed, her voice breaking with fury.

John stood frozen, the speed of it all crashing over him. The accusations, the betrayal — it was too much. His heart ached, and the bitterness in Sarah's voice echoed in his mind.

Sensing his turmoil, Maria gently touched his arm. "Come on," she said quietly………

"Let's take a walk." She suggested to him.

And with that, they stepped away, leaving the deception behind them.

They grabbed a coffee and something to eat from the small booth on the street and sat on a worn wooden bench nearby. The evening was calm, the air crisp with a hint of the approaching night. The park stretched around them, in front of them they could see the beach, bathed in soft golden light, the fading sun casting long, warm shadows across the path. The trees stood tall, their branches swaying gently in the breeze, as though the world itself was sighing with relief. Lights flickered to life overhead, illuminating the park in a soft glow, casting a peaceful, almost magical quality over everything. The distant sound of children's laughter mixed with the gentle rustling of leaves, filling the air with the pulse of life.

The little food truck, where they had picked up their meal, was tucked in a quiet corner of the park, surrounded by a patch of lush green grass, and the scent of freshly made hotdogs mingled with the earthy aroma of the evening. People wandered past, lost in their own worlds, some couples, some alone, all caught in the warmth of the setting sun. Yet, amidst the beauty of it all, John sat in stillness, distant, his eyes clouded, his thoughts clearly far from the peaceful surroundings.

Maria glanced at him, noticing how the lines on his face had deepened, how his shoulders seemed to bear a load heavier than the simple moment they shared. The rays that bathed the park seemed to glow around her, but it barely touched him. His eyes were fixed on the ground, his expression tight, his mind clearly still tangled in the betrayal and disappointment from earlier.

Sarah's words, the accusations, the stress of the situation—it all lingered with him, like a bitter taste in his mouth that he could not shake. He was disappointed, not just in Sarah, but in everything. In himself. In the way things had turned out. In the choices they had all made. The light around them did not seem to matter to him anymore, as though the world had gone grey.

Maria took a slow breath, watching the way the light caught in his hair, how the shadows seemed to lengthen across his face, as if even the park was trying to give him space to think. She could sense the heaviness in him, and despite the beautiful evening unfolding around them, she sat with him to let go of whatever burden he carried.

She turned slightly toward him, her voice soft but clear, breaking through the silence that hung between them. "John," she began, her words gentle, the warmth of the evening and the fading sunlight wrapping around her. "I know you are carrying so much right now. But you don't have to do it alone…I suppose you liked her. Maybe that's why you are so shaken," she said, her gaze drifting to the pavement.

John's eyes stayed with the crowd, his face darkening. "Yes," he muttered.

"I liked her. I even thought about asking her out one day. But now… seeing this… it's hard to believe. After everything, she feels nothing. No guilt. Not even a hint."

The city buzzed around them, but his mind was far from the noise. His words spilled out. "It's dangerous… when people shut off their conscience, become like machines. They can't tell right from wrong anymore."

Maria looked at him, then turned her attention to the street ahead. The sounds of life around them seemed to grow quieter as she spoke…. "Well said… but look around you, John."

Her eyes scanned the street, and the world seemed to pause. The passing strangers— families walking hand in hand, children laughing as they played in the sand on the nearby beach.

Maria asked him, meaningfully… "What do you see, John?"

John shifted, his eyes sweeping over the people, still lost in the cloud of his thoughts.

"I see people… a lot of people," he said, his stare distant.

She nodded slowly, her eyes widening as she watched him. "But look closer," she urged. "You know, when you are watching a movie, you see everything happening, and you can tell what is right, what is wrong. You say, 'Why are they doing that? Why not do what is right?'"

She let her words settle in the air before continuing. "In every situation, John… imagine you are just a viewer. Look at them… do you see that family and the other one with the kids playing in the sand?"

Maria's eyes lingered on the families, "One of those families," she continued, "is Black, and the other is White. They don't even speak to each other, just lost in their own world. They don't notice that their children are playing together."

She paused, her mind never leaving the scene. "But wait," she added after a moment.

A minute or two pass, and the mother of the white boy gets up and walks over to him. She pulls him aside, scolds him, tells him, "You shouldn't be playing with that child, because he's Black. It does not fit our image" ……. Then the mother of the Black boy does the same. She pulls him away and tells him … "Don't play with that child, they are not like us, they are dangerous." With this, Maria tried to make more sense in her explanation.

John stood there, his gaze fixed on the scene unfolding before them. The words were strong. The families remained unaware, continuing in their own worlds, oblivious to the consequences of their actions.

"That's pathetic," John said softly.

Maria nodded, her eyes unwavering, her voice calm but carrying a quiet strength.

"I know…but it's not the world that forces us into these situations. It's us, John. We choose to place ourselves in these moments, that alter our perception, even from childhood. Our egos—they are the ones that do this to us."

She turned to face him, her eyes searching his. "What do you see now, John?"

John's eyes followed her direction.

"That man in the suit," she asked softly. "He's probably too busy to even finish his coffee. Maybe he's late for some important meeting."

John nodded, his thoughts connecting as he looked at the man. But Maria was not finished.

"He's caught up in a cycle, John. He sees money as the goal. He thinks it's his to control. But what he does not see—what he does not understand—is that the money is controlling him. Not the other way around."

Maria shifted her focus, her attention now falling on an older couple sitting on a nearby bench. Their hands were intertwined, a quiet display of love that had stood the test of time.

"And then, look at them," she said, her voice full of warmth. "That old couple. Still holding hands. It's rare, isn't it? You don't see it often. But when you do… it's beautiful. The kind of love that doesn't need words. The kind of love that lasts."

John's eyes locked onto hers…. "I get your point!"

Maria's expression soft and knowing. "I know."

Without another word, John pulled her close, wrapping his arms around her in a tight embrace. "Thank you," he whispered, his words barely audible. "I'm really sad for Sarah."

"She's a good person," he continued, strained. "But she doesn't see it. And as long as she refuses to, all the effort, all the words from everyone—it will not change a thing."

Maria placed her hand on his back. "Exactly."

Before she could say another word, she heard the distant roar of a motorcycle, growing louder by the second.

In a heartbeat, the figure on the back pulled a gun, and everything seemed to freeze. Maria's breath caught in her chest as the first shots rang out, echoing in the broken peace.

John reacted in an instant, grabbing Maria and pulling her to the ground, shielding her with his body. His hand fumbled for his gun, without hesitating, he fired back, the world spinning around them in a blur of gunshots and panic.

The motorcycle jerked away, disappearing into the distance as quickly as it had arrived. The street, once calm, erupted into mayhem. John's hands were trembling as he pushed himself up, scanning the area. His eyes darted to Maria, and his voice was low, almost desperate. "Are you okay?"

Maria nodded, her eyes wide with shock, but when she looked down at him, she saw the bloodstain seeping through his shirt, dark and ominous.

A silence fell between them, how had the serenity been shattered so easily?

"Are you okay?" John asked, once again with concern.

"Yeah, I'm fine," she replied quickly. "John, you're bleeding. Are you sure you're alright?"

"I'm fine," he reassured her, his voice was steady but strained. "Don't worry about me."

She hesitated, a feeling of worry crossing her face, as they both took a deep breath and began calming each other down. The uncertainty around them, the panic everywhere slowly began to dissipate as the people on the street and the beach found their own rhythm of reassurance.

But across the globe, Samara and Antonio arrived in Brazil, already entering her son Gabriel's house. That's when Antonio received an urgent call.

"Excuse me, ma'am," Antonio said quietly, his tone polite but urgent.

"Let's hope there are no problems," Samara replied, firmly. She glanced at him for a moment before stepping inside, her arrival warmly received. Antonio nodded, stepping aside, his focus already shifting to the next matter at hand.

"Yes, I'm listening," Antonio said.

On the other line, the two men from the motorcycle greeted him.

"Hello," they said, but their tone was defeated.

"What's going on? Did you finish the job?" Antonio's voice remained controlled, though there was an edge to it.

"No, boss. There was someone else with him, and we could not finish him off," they replied, frustrated.

"We acted too fast," one of them added, the guilt clear in his words.

Antonio's venom released. "Idiots," he muttered under his breath. "Useless fools!" He slammed the phone down, his fingers trembling slightly. The two men continued to argue on the other end, but it was pointless now. Antonio's mind was already moving elsewhere. He entered the house, walking with steady steps, his jaw clenched as he tried to suppress the rising tension in his chest.

Maria and John had just entered his apartment. The door clicked shut softly behind them. Maria gently supported John, her arm around his waist, guiding him toward the kitchen. He winced slightly, his face pale from the blood loss, but tried to seem unaffected.

"Why didn't we go to the hospital?" Maria asked, concerned as she helped him sit down on the highchair next to the kitchen counter.

John leaned back, his hand still pressed to his side, trying to hold it together.

"I told you, I don't like hospitals," he replied through clenched teeth. He tried to be calm, but the strain was clear in his eyes.

Maria looked at him closely, her anxiety deepening. She could see the blood pooling through his shirt, staining the fabric.

"Look at how much you're bleeding," she said, before moving quickly to grab the first aid kit from the shelf above.

John's teeth gritted, fighting back the pain. "If you could be a little more careful, please… It would be better."

Maria paused and nodded, without a word, her movements gentle as she opened the first aid kit. She moved closer, kneeling beside him, and began cleaning the wound with careful precision. The smell of alcohol mixed with the sterile scent of the kit, filling the air. John winced, but the touch of her hands—steady, calm— kept him grounded. The pain was sharp, but there was something comforting about the way she cared for him. She wiped the blood away; her concentration fixed on the wound as she worked.

"It's not too deep," she said continuing... "It's more like a big cut... The bullet must have just grazed you."

John exhaled sharply, his muscles tensing as the sensation of cool alcohol met the rawness of the wound. He closed his eyes for a moment, the pain fading just slightly under her gentle touch. Maria's hands were steady, almost tender as she cleaned him up, each movement precise and purposeful.

Outside the apartment, the world continued as it always did. But in their small, quiet space, something sparkled. In that moment, the bond between them grew stronger. The chaos of the world outside seemed distant, far removed from the intimacy of the moment. Maria finished cleaning the wound, her hands still hovering near him. She looked up at him, her eyes searching his face, waiting for some sign of reassurance. John met her gaze, his lips curling into a faint, pained smile. "I'll survive," he said, with more vulnerability than before.

"You're still lucky," she said, soft but knowing.

He glanced at her, a playful hint in his eyes.

"You too," he replied, a lightness in his tone that didn't quite match the gravity of the situation.

"Alright, then," she said, her hands already reaching for the bandages. "Stand up."

She worked with careful precision, wrapping the cloth around his back.

"Yeah," he answered, a smile tugging at his lips, despite the pain, carrying an edge of irony. "After all, that bullet could've hit you."

She paused, her fingers gently pressing against the wound. "Hmm, really?" she murmured, as if the thought of him being hurt hit her a little too hard.

"Ow, ow, alright," he winced, trying to laugh it off. "I'm just joking."

When she finished bandaging him, she stepped back, giving him space to breathe. He looked at her, gratitude in his eyes, muttering a quiet thank you before turning to his room. Inside, he rifled through his closet, searching for a shirt that felt right—but none of them did. Everything felt too tight, too uncomfortable.

Just then, little John appeared at the door, his small body moving gracefully toward him. The cat, as if sensing his unease, purred, rubbing against his legs. The warmth of the gesture caught him off guard. Little John hopped up onto the bed, making himself comfortable at the foot, curling into a little ball. He began to lick his paws, his movements slow, deliberate—a quiet, grounding presence in the room. It was simple, but in that moment, it was everything.

"So, that's where you're sleeping?" John asked with a mix of teasing and curiosity as he looked at him. "I see... and where's your friend the one you've been ignoring me for?" He shook his head, slipping on the shirt he had finally chosen, before walking out of his room.

The cold hit him as he stepped into the hallway, and there, on the couch, he saw Maria asleep. He whispered to himself, "Of course, she's asleep..." Stepping closer, looking down at her, tracing the peaceful curve of her face. It was as if her beauty made the world around him disappear, as though she existed in a place beyond this time.

Without thinking, he carefully lifted her into his arms. The sharp sting from his own wound flared up, but he pushed the pain away. His focus was only on her. Carrying her gently to his room, his movements soft, as if she were something precious, something fragile. He laid her down on the bed, careful not to disturb her too much.

Maria shifted slightly, and with a soft, feline grace, she began to nuzzle the pillow, just like a cat would, her face moving in a rhythmic pattern. After a few moments, she relaxed into the bed and fell into a deep, peaceful sleep.

John watched her for a moment, a soft smile forming on his lips. He glanced over at little John, who was still lounging nearby. "That's why you two understand each other, huh?" he said, a playful gleam in his eyes. "Maybe, in a past life, she was a cat too…… a beautiful cat"

Chapter 7

The next morning in Rio de Janeiro, while everyone was having breakfast in Gabriel's large estate garden, Lilly, his girlfriend, brought up the topic.

"So, Samara, what brings you here, and how long do you plan to stay?" She asked with a little pride.

Gabriel immediately gave her a stern look, but Samara was not uncomfortable at all. She was not worried about anyone or anything.

"Let's just say I'll be staying for a while," Samara replied.

"I have been so busy and want to spend more time with my son. Now, excuse me, I've got some work to do. I have many acquaintances here and need to catch up with everyone." She then left them to have breakfast in peace.

Lilly turned to Gabriel, her voice sharp. "Seriously? After three years, not once did she call to ask how you were or if you were okay, and now she shows up from Miami. What, did she cause some trouble there and that's why she is here now?" Her words, full of judgment.

Gabriel's expression darkened, and he looked at her seriously.

"Will you stop?" he said quietly. "After everything… Have some respect. She may not be perfect, but she's, my mother."

He stood up from the table. "Anyway, it doesn't matter why she is here. Enjoy your breakfast."

Lily had not paid any attention to his words. Instead, she began to relax after he left, her body unwinding.

Back in Miami, early morning light bathed the cemetery in soft hues. Maria stood still in front of her grandmother's grave, her thoughts distant. The air was cool, but the sun was already climbing, casting a beautiful glow that made the surroundings feel oddly serene. Suddenly, John appeared beside her, moving quietly as if he had stepped out of the shadows. Maria startled, her eyes meeting his as he looked at the gravestone.

"Camila and Gloria de Perez," he read from the tombstone. "Who were they?" He questioned.

Maria's gaze flickered over to him. "You followed me?" she asked, confusion in her words. "But why?" She added.

"I wanted you safe," he said, almost reluctantly. "But I never imagined you'd come here."

They shared a moment of silence, the only sound the distant rustle of leaves in the breeze. After a beat, they moved towards Lee's grave. The sun now fully risen, casting its warm light on the stone as John placed his hand gently on the stone.

"Rest in peace, Uncle," he murmured.

Maria stood for a moment, her fingers lightly grazing the cold grave.

"Oh, Lee," she whispered softly, a sadness in her face.

As they waited, Maria began to speak. "Camila was a kind woman, old but full of warmth, and Gloria… she was always challenging, always chasing something more. They were close to your uncle. That is how I knew them."

John's expression softened with sympathy. "What happened to them?" he asked, quieter now, as if afraid to disturb the delicate air around them.

Maria exhaled slowly, her mind distant. "Someone planted a bomb in their house," she said, her words steady. "It exploded while they were inside."

John's face tightened with shock, but he didn't interrupt her. Maria continued, her words becoming a quiet reflection of the past.

"It was someone from Samara's side," she added, almost as if she was still trying to piece it all together. "Samara made the call."

"Wait, wait…" John's voice broke through the silence, his expression shifting. "Are we talking about the same Samara?"

Maria paused, she nodded slowly. "Yes… I'm sorry I didn't tell you earlier. But I was not sure you remembered them."

John looked off into the distance, as if the memory was crawling back into his mind, fighting to surface.

He spoke again, more thoughtfully. "I remember. Vaguely, they lived near my uncle's street. I was a kid, but I remember them. The old woman made very nice cookies, the whole street used to smell so good, it was amazing. And the girl... wild, like a storm. Never stayed still, always chasing the light. Always moving."

Maria let out a soft sigh, her eyes softening as she remembered them. "Yes... Sunlight seemed to follow her everywhere."

John shook his head, still lost in the memory. "So, it's them... I can't believe it. I'm so sorry. I never knew what happened to them."

Maria felt her chest tighten, but she didn't let it show. She had to hold on to the truth, to the facts. "It's... it's a long story. But I'm glad you remember. I didn't think you would. It's strange, you know? How the past sometimes finds its way back to you."

John met her thoughts, his words settling between them. "And Samara? So, she was the one who did it?"

Maria nodded, "Yes. She did it. And your uncle, he... he made sure she paid for it. For what she did to them. He was the one who put her in prison."

The wind seemed to grow quiet, like the street around them was waiting for the next piece of the story. John's jaw clenched as he looked away, processing the information. "How? She was dangerous... How did he manage to put her away?"

Maria heard him, but she didn't answer right away. "He knew how to handle people like her. He had his ways, his connections. When someone did something like that... there was no escape."

The tension lingered, and in the quiet, their shared history seemed to press closer, like it was still alive, still wrapping around their feet.

John headed to the station, while Maria made her way to the café, the one she and his uncle used to visit. It felt like a quiet refuge, a place where memories lived. Back at the police station, everyone was stunned by the news. Sarah, an insider working for one of the biggest criminals they thought was long dead. It was a revelation that shook them to their core. But the real problem was that no one had the slightest clue where Samara was now. Everyone felt uneasy. John spoke to the captain, recounting everything he had overheard from Sarah's conversation. They all sat in silence for a moment, trying to process the magnitude of it. But the truth was stark—they could not do anything. Samara had already left the country.

Frustrated, John tightened his grip around the edge of the table. "We can't just sit here and wait. I'm going to Brazil. I'll find her. I'll expose Samara." His voice was determined.

His uncle had caught her and put her in prison once before, he knew he could do the same. The risk was high, but what the captain didn't know was that John was not alone. And John was not about to give the captain any say in it. He told him, no debate, he was going no matter what.

Afterward, he headed straight to the cafe where Maria was. As he walked in, he saw her sitting at the corner of the table, sipping tea and reading a book. The scene was calm, almost surreal in the midst of everything going on.

"Interesting!" he said, taking a seat beside her. "I didn't know you liked to read. You don't seem like the type."

Maria glanced at him, a playful curiosity in her eyes. "Interesting! What type do I seem like then?"

John chuckled. "Well, I'd say you have more of a witch vibe." He leaned back slightly, amused.

Maria didn't miss a beat. "Of course, I'm a witch." She stretched out her hand and playfully tapped him in the spot where it would sting the most. "I know if I hit you here, it'll hurt, right?"

John laughed, holding up his hands in surrender. "Alright, alright! Enough with the witch jokes! … I've got news," looking at her seriously. "We're going to Brazil."

For a moment, Maria didn't know how to react. "We're going to Brazil?" she repeated, still trying to grasp what he was saying.

"Yes!" he replied, a little too enthusiastically.

"Bravo! Making decisions without me," she teased, her tone holding just a hint of annoyance.

"Oh, sorry," he said quickly, realising her irritation. "I thought you'd come with me since I'm going anyway. But of course, you can always go back to Manchester, if you want."

Maria gave him a bemused, almost amused look. "And leave you to have all the fun alone?"

"I knew it," he said with a knowing smile. "I knew you'd come."

"You might have known," she replied with a raised brow.

"But don't forget, manners are important," she added with a playful edge to her voice, her gaze loosening.

She then reached into her purse, pulled out the money, and placed it gently on the table for the tea. "Can't forget those details," she said with a sly smile.

"When do we leave?" she asked, standing up and ready to go.

"Now!" he said, grinning, his impatience palpable.

Maria looked at him, a smile playing on her lips. "I do like the way you surprise people."

With that, she turned to leave, her steps light and purposeful.

Before everything, they made sure little John was taken care of. He was left with one of John's oldest friends, someone who had a deep love for animals. As the sun began to dip beneath the horizon, they began their journey. Even though John was fully aware that everything in Brazil would be cutthroat and dangerous, he couldn't shake the feeling that he needed Maria by his side. There was something about her that kept him grounded, something in her that reminded him of his uncle, and that memory, though bittersweet, was a comfort.

Chapter 8

The next morning, the pulse of Rio de Janeiro greeted them. For Maria, this was an entirely new world—one she had only heard about in stories, but now it was alive around her. She marvelled at the way people lived there—simple, free, without expectations or pretence. It was a rhythm of life that she had never known, and it called to her in a way she couldn't explain. The vibrant streets, the sounds of life echoing through the air, and the scent of the sea and flowers filled every corner of her mind.

For a couple of days, they revelled in the freedom that Rio seemed to offer—a freedom they both craved in different ways. John showed her pictures of his parents, leading her to the quiet graves where they were buried. They stayed with a friend of John's, a man whose home was humble, but Maria felt a strange peace there, a comfort in its simplicity. The two of them found joy in the smallest things—a shared cup of coffee, the quiet moments spent in the warmth of the sun, the sound of the waves crashing against the shore.

John, for all his tough exterior, found himself constantly in awe of how Maria seemed to find beauty in things that others would overlook. She saw magic in the everyday, a magic that he had long since forgotten. As they sat together, talking about nothing in particular, John felt a shift. The way she looked at the world was so different from his own—it was as if everything was new and worth seeing for the first time. It reminded him of a time when he, too, saw the world with fresh eyes.

One evening, they ventured out to a street race—an event that had them both electrically captivated. As the race went on, John couldn't help but notice how Maria remained calm. They found themselves in a place where people from all walks of life had gathered, hoping to find some trace of Samara Cabal. They kept to themselves, staying quiet and unobtrusive, knowing that drawing attention would do them no good. They were not sure where to look, and Rio de Janeiro was a vast, dangerous city—beautiful, yes, but as treacherous as it was stunning. Every corner seemed to have its own rules, its own set of unspoken laws that had to be followed.

The evening buzzed with noise. The streets pulsed with the hum of powerful car engines and the low murmur of excited people. John's friend had brought them here, knowing many of the faces in the crowd. But they kept their connection a secret, keeping a low profile.

"Interesting place," Maria said softly, her eyes scanning the surroundings with careful attention. She took in everything—the crowd, the energy, the subtle tension in the atmosphere. The spirit within the city had started to stir, and the stakes were getting high. Maria joined the race, and she won. Then it was John's turn, and he, too, claimed victory. But then came a race that was longer, harder, with even bigger stakes. Not everyone dared to take part in this one, as there were no rules. Whoever won, by any means necessary, would be declared the victor. The wager was their own cars, plus an additional ten thousand each.

Maria and John felt a twinge of concern—they were not racing in their own cars, but in their friends'—despite the risk, they joined. Five people entered, meaning fifty thousand was on the line, along with whatever car remained at the end. And yes, these were the regulars of the scene, the ones who lived for the rush.

In first place was Caio, a legend in this world. He had won nearly everything, his reputation preceding him. In second was Renan, also a fierce competitor, but tonight, she had already conceded a race to Maria, and now she was eager to prove herself again. In third was Rafael, once admired by everyone, though now he only raced occasionally. Yet, despite the years, he was still formidable.

Then there were John and Maria, trailing behind. They were just getting warmed up, curious about the competition and the people, but careful not to stand out too much.

The race began, the road stretched before them, narrow and winding, carved through the rugged mountains that loomed over Rio. The city lights below flickered like scattered stars, but up here, on the twisting, dangerous roads, the night felt alive with threat and promise. The mountain slopes were steep and jagged, and the curves of the road were sharp, a real test for both man and machine. Every twist seemed to hold a challenge—one wrong turn, and it could mean a crash. Yet, no one stopped. The engines roared to life, cutting through the dark like beasts in pursuit. The air was filled with the smell of burning rubber, and the distant hum of the city could not drown out the pounding heartbeats of those racing beneath the stars.

It was dangerous, yes. But in Rio, danger had its own kind of beauty, a seductive, wild energy that only those who knew the city could understand. The race had begun, and as expected, Caio took the lead. Behind him were Rafael and John, with Maria and Renan trailing at the back. But it didn't take long for things to shift. Maria and John were suddenly in the lead, followed by Rafael, Renan, and Caio, who seemed to falter, falling to the back. But Caio was not the type to just accept defeat, like the others. He started playing dirty, trying to force his way past anyone he could. The roads were treacherous, a real challenge for anyone daring enough to race here. Still, everyone pushed forward, each trying to stay ahead in this savage, dangerous game.

Positions shifted constantly—first one ahead, then another. In the chaos, Caio made a move. On the return leg, he shoved Rafael off the road. Rafael's car flipped, rolling across the path and landing on its roof, smoke rising from the wreck.

Maria and John, now in the lead, watched the disaster unfold. Their eyes met for just a moment, and in that brief exchange, they understood each other. Without hesitation, John pressed on, but Maria, her instinct kicking in, turned the car around, heading straight for Rafael.

Caio and Renan laughed, thinking they had won. But then, at the edge of victory, John overtook them, leaving them just behind. Caio realised that if he could push Renan off the road, maybe John would do what Maria had done—turn back to help. And that's exactly what he did. He shoved Renan out of the way, sending her car spinning.

John saw this and immediately made a sharp turn, heading straight for Renan's spinning car. He swerved close, trying to catch up, aiming to stop her from crashing into a building up ahead. He did everything he could to slow her down, as she just narrowly avoided a building. And in that split second, Caio crossed the finish line.

He won.

The crowd was pumped, but for Maria and John, it didn't seem to matter. John, having managed to prevent a crash with Renan, was now focused on the aftermath of the mess. Maria, meanwhile, was not worried about what happened with the race—her focus was entirely on Rafael. The sight of his car smoking, more and more with every second, pushed her into action. She had known the danger. She didn't hesitate. Her heart raced as she slammed the brakes and jumped out of the car. The metallic scent of smoke was thick in the air, and the heat radiated off the burning vehicle.

Rafael, visibly shaken, struggled in his seat, but his door was jammed. The smoke grew thicker, and panic set in for him. Maria didn't waste a moment, despite him barely understanding her words in English. Her calm yet urgent tone broke through his fear. "I'll get you out, just stay calm," she said, trying to assure him.

She was quick. His leg was caught, twisted in a way that made the escape harder, but managed to urgently free him, dragging him away from the wreck. The city seemed to disappear in those few moments, and Maria felt a sense of responsibility, as if everything depended on this rescue. She gritted her teeth, her muscles straining as she pulled Rafael toward her own car, not caring that he was heavier than she expected.

John had stopped, his heart pounding, watching as Maria took the risk. Behind them, Rafael's car exploded in a violent burst, sending a wave of heat through the air.

Later, when they returned, the streets of Rio felt almost surreal, just like a dream everything was soon forgotten. People were cheering, the energy bursting everywhere, but for Maria and John, it felt like they were in a different space. The loud, reckless thrill of the race had passed, but the unease clung to them.

Maria drove silently, her face tight, while John's anger was palpable. His grip on the steering wheel tightened, the rage boiling inside of him from the close call. He didn't want to show it, but the thought that they had come so close to losing someone was too much to bear. He shot Maria a look, his eyes sharp with frustration, but Maria didn't react. She met his eyes, feeling his anger but trying to stay composed. She didn't want to let it show, didn't want things to escalate.

Renan's voice cut through the tension, a small, trembling … Thank you. She stepped out of the car, her face pale, still shaken from the near-death experience.

John's voice was steady, though there was a quiet storm in his words. "It's alright. Just breathe, you are safe now."

The tension between John and Caio was building up, and it reached it's peak when John saw Caio celebrating, surrounded by others who were applauding his victory. John's anger was strong as he locked eyes with Maria again, who was still helping Rafael in the car. She noticed his frustration but didn't have time to intervene.

Quickly, she turned to Renan, instructing her to take Rafael to the hospital, his injuries severe—broken ribs and a fractured leg. Maria's concern was obvious, but there was no time to waste. Renan hesitated but nodded, and Maria swiftly moved to follow John, sensing that something was about to happen. As John walked toward Caio, the laughter and cheers of the group only made him more agitated. Caio noticed John coming and greeted him with a mocking smile. "What's up, man? You look like you are still upset about losing, huh?" His words were met with laughter from the others, adding to John's fury. But John didn't hesitate. Without waiting for Caio to even take a sip from his beer, John grabbed the bottle right out of his hand and threw it to the ground, shattering it into pieces. The group fell silent instantly, taken aback by his sudden aggression. John wasted no time. With a swift motion, he grabbed Caio by the arm, twisting it behind his back and pushing him roughly toward the hood of his car. Caio winced, the pain shooting through him as John pressed harder.

Caio's face which was contorting with pain, could not do anything but grunt in agony. The sudden shift in power had everyone frozen, unsure of how to react. It was clear that John had lost all patience, and Caio's mocking attitude had pushed him over the edge. The atmosphere was strong, charged with raw emotion. John's actions spoke louder than any words could, and Caio's defiance began to fade under the pressure. The celebration that had been so loud moments ago was now a hushed silence, as everyone waited for what would happen next.

The stress grew, as everyone around John and Caio pulled out their weapons, aiming them directly at John. But John remained unfazed, his focus still entirely on Caio. His grip tightened on

Caio's arm, and he hissed in Portuguese, "Such a pitiful creature, is this what you call a victory, you pathetic loser?"

Before anything could escalate further, Maria rushed forward, her voice sharp and commanding. "Hey, hey! Put the weapons down! We don't want any trouble!" she shouted, her eyes scanning the crowd. She turned to John, pulling him away from Caio and trying to calm him down.

"Come on, enough! Stop! Do you really think talking to him like this will change anything?" she said, her voice filled with both concern and authority.

John hesitated, his anger still simmering, but at Maria's words, he released Caio's arm and turned toward her. Maria, her stare firm, spoke again, "Now put the guns down! Like I said, we don't want any problems!"

Caio, still nursing his twisted arm, quickly stood up and tried to regain control of the situation. He stood tall, looking around at the group of men, trying to appear nonchalant.

"Guys, guys! Calm down! Clearly, these people are new here and don't know who they are dealing with," he said, trying to brush it off.

One of the men, seeing Caio's attempt to regain his composure, handed him a fresh bottle of beer, and Caio cracked it open with a smug grin.

"Let's go," Maria said to John, looking at him with calm eyes.

But just as they turned to leave, Caio's voice rang out, sharp and challenging. "Hey, hey! Where do you think you are going?" he called, a smirk tugging at the corner of his lips.

Maria stopped and turned to face him. "You've got the money, the cars—we're square," she said, trying to keep the situation from escalating. She motioned to John, signalling that it was time to go, but as they began to walk away, the men raised their guns again, pointing them at the pair.

"Don't think you're getting away so easily," one of the men sneered.

John's voice cut through. "We warned you, not once but twice. I don't think you want to test us."

Laughter broke out from the group, a taunting sound that only fuelled the fire further. Caio's smug expression remained as he spoke again.

"So, you think you are something special now? You come in here, win a few races, and think that makes you a big deal?"

Maria exchanged a quick glance with John. Her eyes speaking volumes, so John could understand exactly what to do. Maria stepped forward, closing the gap between her and Caio. She met his face unflinching.

"You know, I think that you think the world is at your feet," looking him in the eyes, and then suddenly lowering her gaze to his feet.

He laughed and said, "Oh, sweetheart, the world really is at my feet," then started speaking loudly, laughing, and looking at his friends.

"And it's so alive, alive, alive." Everyone started laughing again. Then he came over to her and asked: "And do you want to see how alive the world is at my feet?"

Maria looked at him with interest, which made him think that she was intrigued. But after a second, she said, "You know, an interesting question is spinning in my head," then whispered to him: "I was thinking, what would happen to all that world at your feet, if you didn't have those feet at all?"

He gave a surprised look, but Maria didn't wait. In one swift move, she grabbed the gun from his hands, and without a moment's notice, fired. The shot rang out, echoing through the air, as the bullet slammed into his legs. The man staggered back, collapsing to the ground in pain, before anyone could even react, John was on the move.

In a fluid swift motion, he disarmed one of the men who had tried to rush him. His grip was firm as he twisted the weapon out of the man's hand, then with quick, brutal movement, slammed the butt of the gun into his opponent's face, knocking him unconscious. Maria, always in sync with him, was already in action, firing at the legs of another man who had lunged at her. Her aim was precise, the shot ringing out sharply, causing him to drop to the floor, gripping his leg in agony.

The two of them moved like a coordinated machine, the shots firing out in rapid succession, the air crackling with flashes. With the sound of bullets flying and men screaming in pain, they kept moving, never giving their enemies a chance to recover. But soon enough, their ammo ran out. The sharp, metallic sound of empty chambers sounded in the silence between the gunfire. There was no time to reload.

With no more bullets to fire, the fight shifted to pure hand-to-hand combat. John was first to strike, his fist slamming into the jaw of one of the attackers with a sickening crack. He followed up with a swift kick to another man's ribs, sending him crashing into a nearby table. Maria was not far behind—she twisted and kicked, her legs fluid like a dancer, but the strikes were calculated and precise. A hard elbow to the gut sent one of their attackers reeling, while a quick uppercut knocked another out cold.

They were moving faster than the men could keep up, a blur of calculated force and sheer survival. The combat was ruthless and brutal, each punch and kick landing with bone-shattering force. But the chaos was not over. As the last of their attackers fell, the screech of police sirens sliced through the air, growing louder by the second.

Maria froze, a brief flicker of surprise crossing her face. She had expected something else—more time, perhaps—but not this. John settled the confusion, sharp and commanding. "Stay calm. I called them," he said, his tone as cold as steel.

Before they could even process what was happening, those who were still standing were fleeing, scrambling in all directions. Panic ensued, the sound of footsteps pounding the pavement outside grew louder as they tried to escape. But not everyone made it. The police arrived in full force, blocking the exits, and those who could not flee were quickly caught.

John and Maria were among those caught. Handcuffed and shoved into separate cars, they were taken to the police station. The clatter of doors slamming shut echoing down the narrow halls as they were thrown into cells. It was not the quiet evening they had hoped for. It was chaos, a mixture of uncertainty and adrenaline.

John and Maria were placed together in a cell, but not alone, surrounded by strangers, the smell of sweat, cheap cologne, and stale air filled the space. The walls were cold and unyielding, the distant murmur of other prisoners muffling the sounds of the jail. Despite everything, Maria stayed composed. Her eyes moved methodically across the room, while John stood tall, his presence as commanding as ever. They weren't defeated. Not yet.

The small, dimly lit cell felt tight. Maria shifted uncomfortably, her mind racing through a thousand thoughts, yet none of them clear. The silence between her and John was more intense than the chaos of the night before. She stared at the wall, fingers nervously tracing patterns on her jacket. Finally, she broke the quiet.

"I can't believe this, John. Seriously?" she said, tinged with disbelief. Her gaze was sharp, filled with frustration.

John, leaning back against the cold metal bars, barely glanced at her. He was calm, too calm for the situation.

"Relax," he interrupted her, his tone reassuring. "They will check us out. Once they see who I am, they will release us." His words were meant to calm, but his statement didn't quite settle in the room.

She snapped her head toward him brows furrowed in disbelief. "You are the police man, not me!"

"But you're with me, right?" His hands moved to her shoulders, steadying her, his eyes meeting hers. "So don't worry. We will not be here long." His words hung between them, a promise that Maria didn't fully believe but hoped was true. She nodded slowly, trying to find peace in his certainty, but deep down, the fear still gnawed at her.

Chapter 9

The next day, Gabriel sat across the table from a group of his associates, their faces hard and unreadable in the plush, overly grandiose room of the mansion. The discussion was cold and calculated, the topic at hand: drugs. How quickly they moved, how easily they were traded.

"Well," one of the men said, leaning forward with an inquisitive look.

"I hear that your mother is here. She met my father. Is she planning to stay around?"

His tone was casual, but there was an underlying curiosity.

Gabriel didn't even flinch, his eyes piercing as he gave his response.

"I don't know. But if you are that interested, you can ask her yourself." His words were steady, almost bored, as though he were discussing the weather.

The other man shook his head, a slight laugh escaping him. "No, no. I'm not looking to get involved with your mother."

Gabriel smiled, but it was not kind. "Good. Because I don't think she wants to get involved with any of you either."

The room fell quiet for a moment, but then Gabriel leaned back in his chair, with an almost mocking tone said, "So, are we done here?"

Everyone at the table stood, nodding in agreement, their business concluded. Gabriel stood too, waiting for them to file out, leaving him alone with his thoughts. After coming home, Gabriel found his girlfriend, Lilly, smashing everything she could get her hands on in the living room. He calmly walked over to her.

"What are you doing? What's going on?" he asked, stopping her and gently placing his hands on her shoulders. "Are you high?"

She shrugged him off, snapping at him, "Am I high? Yeah, damn it, I'm high. But it's not the drugs, Gabriel. It's my anger toward your mother."

She turned to one of the rooms, sitting there, almost as if nothing had happened.

Gabriel blinked, surprised. "My mother? What are you talking about? What happened?"

"Go ask her," she shot back. "I'm leaving, because if I stay, I swear I'll kill her."

Gabriel raised an eyebrow, unfazed. "Alright, just don't say anything you'll regret."

Lilly grumbled something under her breath but stormed out. Gabriel, still cool and calm, made his way toward his mother's room. He knocked softly, and when he heard her voice saying to come in, he opened the door. Samara motioned for Antonio to leave and said they would continue later. Gabriel walked to the window and glanced out, his posture easy and relaxed, almost as if he had no care in the world. "Hey, Mom. Just checking, are you here for some fun, messing up the peace for everyone?"

He turned to face her, a soft, almost playful smile on his face. "Relax. Take it easy."

Samara sighed, rolling her eyes. "Messing up the peace for everyone? What are you talking about? Oh, wait, you mean that friend of yours... what is her name? The one you call your girlfriend?"

Gabriel's smile didn't falter, his tone smooth.

"Her name's Lilly, Mom. And if you want to know, she's been helping me make some of the best deals in the business for over three years now."

"Well, then," Samara replied, "That's how it is, huh?"

Gabriel's expression softened, his demeanour completely unbroken. "Yeah, Mom. That's how it is."

Gabriel leaned against the doorframe, his posture casual, but his hands were loosely clenched in his pockets. His eyes were calm, but there was a slight tension beneath the surface that was hard to miss. He studied his mother, taking a slow breath as he let her words sink in.

"So, you kicked everyone out, huh?" he asked, smoothly, like it didn't bother him at all.

"The whole party, with all those junkies, just because you couldn't take it anymore?"

His mother shot him a sharp look, but Gabriel's expression remained unchanged. There was something in the way he spoke that made her uncomfortable. It was like he wasn't reacting the way she expected him to.

"Yeah," she said, a hint of frustration creeping into her tone. "I had enough. It's my house, my rules."

Gabriel's lips curled up into a faint, almost imperceptible smile...

"And what do you mean, exactly?" he asked.

She snapped, "You know exactly what I mean! She's not good for you. I've seen it a thousand times. It's one thing to sell that trash, but it's another to use it. Do you get me?"

Gabriel blinked slowly, his eyes never leaving her face. He took a deep breath and relaxed even more into his stance, looking like he was not in the least bit concerned.

"I don't use anything, mom," he replied. His tone dropped slightly as he added:

"And I don't mind that Lilly does. She knows what she's doing. She's just... living, you know?"

His mother narrowed her eyes at him, clearly not liking how he was defending Lilly.

Gabriel, however, was not fazed. He could feel the stress in her, but his calmness only seemed to make her more agitated.

"Stay out of it, mom," he said with finality. "It's none of your business."

She stared at him, confused and upset, trying to understand why he was so indifferent to her feelings. Gabriel was not even raising his voice—he was just there, comfortable in his own skin, and it bothered her more than anything.

He continued, almost like he was reassuring her, his words cutting through with quiet strength. "I'm glad you're here, really. But if you want respect, you've got to give it, too."

The room seemed to grow quieter, his calmness, the way he stood there with his shoulders loose, almost felt like a challenge to her, as if he were daring her to try and make him feel something he didn't want to feel.

He spoke slowly, as if savouring every word, carefully assessing how it would land with his mother. "Mom let's get one thing straight," he began.

"I'm not standing behind anyone's back. I'm just telling you how things are."

He leaned back slightly, his gaze unwavering, a subtle defiance in his eyes.

"Lilly, besides being the woman I'm with, she's a damn good partner in this business. She knows the game, and she helps me make the kind of money that only comes with a sharpened skill."

He paused for a moment, his eyes shifting briefly to the window.

"Brazil's the perfect place for this," he said. "And let's not forget, everything I've built here… it's not all my doing. A lot of it's on her too. When I look at her, sometimes I swear I'm looking at you. You both share that hunger, that drive to be number one."

His words held a truth in the comparison. The silence that followed was sharp, his mother's face flushing with indignation. "What? Don't compare me to her," she snapped, as she felt betrayed showing the tremor of frustration.

"I have class. She doesn't."

Gabriel, cut her off with quiet authority.

"Enough, Mom. I really don't have time for this." His words, direct.

"I've got work to do. I have already heard that people know you are here. Just enjoy yourself. Don't stir up trouble."

His mother straightened up, her posture rigid, but the strain in her face softened as she exhaled. "Okay, son," she said quietly, the edge in her voice dissipating. "I'm sorry. You're right. I just want what's best for you."

Gabriel leaned forward slightly "Mom, look at me. I am what you always wanted me to be. I'm in charge of one of the most successful drug operations in Rio. You should be proud of me." His words, though grounded in truth, held a strange gentleness.

She looked at him, her eyes still filled with concern.

"But son, don't you want a woman who can give you a family? A mother for your children, not someone who uses drugs?"

Gabriel's rage was real, but he walked toward her with a deliberate calmness. His presence seemed to fill the room, and as he neared Samara, he spoke, voice measured, with something she couldn't ignore.

"Why do you think I want children?" His words dropped like stones in the stillness, and the room seemed to hold its breath. "Let me make it clear, for the last time."

"Because of your dirty games, Gloria is dead. And now, she rests in peace, alongside her grandmother. I became exactly what you always dreamed I would be." His eyes held hers, steady, unyielding. "And do you know why?" He stepped closer, his face hardening with the weight of years of suppressed grief. "After her… I couldn't see myself as anything else."

For a moment, it felt like time stood still. Samara stood frozen, the moment rife with tension. He had said her name. After all these years, he had said it.

Her breath caught, and she took a step toward him, disbelief flooding her voice.

"After all these years, I thought you'd forgotten her?" she asked, with an emotion she could not quite name.

Gabriel halted, his expression unreadable. Looking out the window for a moment and then turning to face her.

"I will never forget her, Mom. Never," he said, the words quiet but final, like a promise he would never break. Without another word, he walked out, his footsteps pulsing in the silence that hung between them. Samara stood there, staring at the empty space where he had been, the truth washing over like a cold wave.

How could he still think of her after all these years? How could he carry her memory like that—like something precious, something undying? Samara's mind raced, struggling to understand. The silence stretched on, heavy with the unanswered question: had Gabriel ever truly forgotten Gloria? Had he really let her go, or had she been with him all along, even in the dark corners of his mind?

It was a question that Samara would never get an answer to. And it haunted her.

At that time, in the police station, the captain tried to look through John's police records at the station, he muttered to himself, "Seriously?" before heading toward the cell where they were held. He told the guards to open the doors in Portuguese, and they all exchanged some words. John and Maria exchanged a glance as they had been waiting all night and nearly the entire morning for someone to release them.

The guards told John to step out, but he insisted that Maria come with him.

The captain allowed it since Maria had no criminal record. Once they were out and in the captain's office, he turned to John and said, "Well, John," speaking in Portuguese, "you have really changed, huh? Seems like you have become a real police man."

John stared at him in confusion, and asked… "Excuse me, do we know each other?"

He paused and then switched to English. "Sorry, let's speak in English, since she doesn't understand Portuguese." He turned to Maria with a smile.

"Oh, yes, of course," the captain continued. "I'm… Don't you remember me? Uncle Pedro, your father's best friend, back in the day. Sure, my English might be a little rusty, but you get me, right?"

"Uncle Pedro?" John said, shocked and delighted. "I can't believe it. You've changed too! Are you a captain now?"

"Yes, over the years I became a captain," Pedro replied. Then, he looked at Maria and asked, "And who is she?"

"She's my friend," John said. "A very good friend."

"Hi, nice to meet you," Pedro greeted her.

"Nice to meet you too," Maria responded.

"So, what brings you here?" Pedro asked. "And what is this mess about the riot last night? We caught a bunch of the punks who have been running wild for a while but could not get them until now. What is your involvement?"

"We didn't want to get involved in any trouble; we were just looking for information" John added. But Maria glanced at him, barely a whisper… "John, stop, don't do this."

"Relax," he said. "We can trust him. I grew up with him."

"Take it easy, girl," his uncle added. "He is like a son to me. So, what is happening?"

"Well, a woman named Samara Cabal is here," John said.

"She's a very dangerous person," John continued, his expression serious. "And she might be connected to my uncle Lee's death."

Pedro was taken aback. "Your uncle is dead? I had no idea. I'm so sorry about your loss."

"Thank you," John replied, his voice filled with determination. "But we're here because of her. We need to get to the bottom of this."

"Alright," Pedro said, nodding. "Give me a couple of days. I'll see what I can do for you."

After their agreement, everyone returned to their duties. John and Maria made their way through the winding streets, heading toward John's friend's place in town—a small, familiar refuge amid the avenues. As they arrived, children from all around the neighbourhood poured out of their homes, drawn by their presence. Maria's face lit up; she loved these moments, playing with the kids, slipping into their carefree world. The afternoon melted with their laughter and games—hide-and-seek, then football—until evening settled in.

As the evening came, Samara and Antonio spoke in hushed tones behind closed doors. Lilly had stopped in the hallway, silently listening in.

"Antonio," Samara's voice was cold and sharp, "today's news overwhelmed me. Sarah's locked away, we must send someone to finish the job." Her eyes glinted with resolve. "Slowly, my business, my life—it'll all be here."

Antonio's confusion wasn't about the plan, but that she spoke English to him instead of Portuguese—an unexpected choice. Before he could respond, she pointed toward the door where a shadow lay. She looked back at him, and he nodded. "Understood, ma'am. I'll handle it."

After hearing everything, Lilly retreated to her room and sank onto the chair, whispering to herself with a mix of disbelief and anger. "What? She's really going to stay here forever? No, I can't let that happen—not without a fight…I won't allow it," she vowed fire setting deep inside her.

Chapter 10

A few days pass, Pedro invited John and Maria to a restaurant tucked away in the mountains, close to the lush tropical rainforest. The moment they arrived; the view stole their breath—like stepping into a secret paradise. Below the restaurant, a river gently wound its way through the towering trees, all drenched in vibrant green, alive and blowing with the breeze. When John and Maria parked their car, they sat still for a heartbeat, drinking in the beauty surrounding them. The calm, the fresh air, the soft sounds of nature—it all wrapped around them like a gentle promise. In that peaceful moment, hope showed, and they felt ready for the conversation ahead with Pedro. What they didn't know was that Antonio was outside too—frozen in place, shocked to see faces he recognised. His pulse spiked. Without thinking, he reached for his phone and called Samara.

"Hello, ma'am!" he said in English, his voice tight with urgency. "You need to come here right away!"

"Antonio, what's going on?" she asked, her tone sharp with concern.

"As you already know, I promised Gabriel I wouldn't interfere. I told him I'd let him deal with Pedro himself." He paused for a beat, trying to steady his breath. "But ma'am… this is urgent. Come immediately. You'll understand everything when you get here."

He hung up without waiting for a reply and started toward the restaurant, each step heavy, his mind racing. Inside, the atmosphere was quiet but charged. John and Maria had just stepped in, scanning the space. Then they saw him—Pedro—sitting calmly at one of the tables.

But he wasn't alone.

Across from Pedro sat someone they couldn't quite make out—the man's back was turned, blocking their view. The two were deep in conversation, but John and Maria couldn't hear a word from where they stood. The distance, the ambient noise… it all blurred their sense of what was unfolding.

What they didn't know was that the man sitting with Pedro was Gabriel.

He had come with one purpose—to persuade Pedro to stay silent. To convince him not to tell his so-called "friends," the ones asking about his mother, that she was here.

Maria told John she was going to the restroom, while he headed straight toward Pedro.

"Look, Pedro," Gabriel said, "I came here on my knees because we've known each other a long time. If I'd left it to my mother, she would have finished you off by now, but still, I stood by you."

"Gabriel," Pedro replied, "I didn't call them here to tell the truth. I called them here to send them away because the boy is close to me. I don't know the girl, but he grew up right before my eyes."

Then Pedro saw John coming with a watchful look.

John sat down with them and said, "Hello" ...to both of them." Turning to Pedro, he added, "Uncle Pedro, how are you? Who's your guest?"

"My name's Gabriel. Nice to meet you," he said, offering his hand.

"John, nice to meet you too," John added.

Gabriel continued, "I'm here because your uncle and I were discussing something work-related." Then he stood up and added, "But we've already covered everything, so I'm leaving now."

As Gabriel turned to leave, his eyes caught John's hand subtly moving toward his weapon. Without hesitation, Gabriel drew his pistol with a quick step and pointed it straight at John's head. His gaze was cold and serious as he said, "That wasn't a good idea."

Pedro immediately stood up, worried, trying to protect John. But Gabriel didn't take his eyes off John and explained, "Now, there's nothing left to do."

John noticed that everyone in the café—both workers and customers—pulled out guns and aimed them at him the moment Gabriel raised his pistol. It was clear they were all Gabriel's people.

Then Gabriel spoke sharply to the crowd, "Put your guns down."

In that moment, things started to shift.

After Gabriel ordered everyone to put their guns down, Maria suddenly appeared, her pistol pressed firmly against Antonio's head. Antonio made a quick gesture to calm everyone, and they slowly returned to their places. Then, Gabriel suddenly felt the cold barrel of Maria's gun pressed against the back of his head, accompanied by the sharp command, "Drop your weapon." At the same moment, Maria pushed Antonio forward just enough for Gabriel to see him clearly—she was still holding Antonio's gun firmly in one hand, while she kept her own weapon pressed to Gabriel's head, controlling them both with deadly precision.

The gun against Gabriel's head didn't shake him—not really. What froze him was that voice, sharp and familiar, cutting through the scene like a knife. His face drained of colour, and the gun slipped from his grip, thudding onto the table. John immediately levelled his weapon at Gabriel, eyes switching briefly toward Maria, never breaking the cold stare locked on Gabriel. "About time," John murmured, "you always show up at the worst moments."

She smiled with a hint of challenge in her voice and said, "And you, as always, trying to have fun without me."

Right as Maria and Gabriel's eyes met, shock hit them both hard. Maria couldn't believe what she was seeing, and neither could Gabriel. Slowly, she lowered her gun's, still pointed at him and Antonio. John, watching this, was clearly confused. "Maria, what are you doing? Are you okay? What's happening?" he asked. Antonio tried to take advantage of the moment, but before he could move, Gabriel snapped his gun off the table and aimed it straight at Antonio—completely ignoring that John might shoot him.

"Don't even think about it," Gabriel said to Antonio, ordering him to lower his weapon. John was confused to see Gabriel pulling his gun and aiming it at his own men. Maria, on the other hand, pleaded, "John, don't do it, please, don't do it, lower your weapon." He didn't lower it, but the disconnect between them was overwhelming. "Maria, what's going on here?" he asked again. "I'll explain everything, John, but please, just lower your weapon now." "No, not until you explain why you're so… why you're in this state, and what the hell is going on here?"

Right then, the restaurant doors swung open, and Samara appeared, moving with a calm, almost regal grace. Behind her, a dozen of her armed men filled the entrance, eyes sharp, weapons ready. Maria's gun was up in an instant, steady and unflinching, aimed straight at Samara. The room froze—then every gun inside the restaurant shifted, trained on Maria and John, fiery and unyielding. But before anyone could act, Gabriel's voice broke the silence, ordering them all to lower their weapons.

Samara slowly slid off her dark sunglasses, revealing eyes wide with disbelief. Her gaze locked onto Maria's, and for a heartbeat, no oxygen could enter her lungs. "You," she whispered, voice trembling with shock. "How? How is this possible? How the hell… how are you alive?"

"John, stay close to me," Maria warned, standing right beside him, knowing things were about to get intense. "Maria, just tell me what's going on," John said.

Maria was sweating, her breath shallow, caught off guard by the unfolding situation. Samara's eyes locked onto her. "So, you're that Maria," she said slowly, then shifted her gaze to John. "And you… you're John……Lee's John…"

"Enough," Gabriel snapped, his voice slicing through the room like a whip. Everyone fell silent. His eyes locked onto Maria.

"How?" he asked, almost breathless. "How are you alive?"

He paused—his chest heaving slightly—then barely whispered, "Gloria."

John's heart skipped. Gloria? The name echoed in his head like thunder. He couldn't move. Couldn't speak. He just stared at her, as if time itself had stopped.

"I saw you," Gabriel continued, his voice trembling now, ripe with emotion. "I saw you with my own eyes. You walked into your house… and minutes later, it exploded."

His hands shook as tears welled up. "So how? How is it possible that you're standing here right now? And where were you? Where have you been all these years?"

Just like that, the walls inside John's mind crumbled. The truth he'd never dared to consider hit him all at once. Maria… was Gloria. The same Gloria they said had died in the fire with her grandmother. The same Gloria tied to the shadows of his fading childhood. The same person he barely remembered—now rising from the ashes of his past.

Maria's eyes locked onto Samara, wide and steady. The room felt alien, the atmosphere shifting with exposed truths. Around them, the workers paused, sensing the change—whispers dying down, eyes flickering between the two women.

"Now I understand," Maria said, calm, and with a cold edge. "But I never thought you'd go this far."

Gabriel couldn't believe the scene in front of him. He glanced at his mother, then back to Maria, the questions burning behind his eyes. "What's going on here?"

The silence stretched longer, heavy with secrets only Maria and Samara shared. Everyone else waited, caught between curiosity and caution.

Maria looked at Samara and said quietly, "Will you tell him, or should I?"

Samara's face twitched with panic. Suddenly, she pulled a gun and tried to shoot Maria—but missed. Chaos exploded. Gunfire rang out, shattering the air. Gabriel jumped in, trying to stop the madness, but ended up firing at his own people. Maria and John scrambled for cover, but a bullet caught Maria in the shoulder. Without a second thought, John grabbed her, and they leapt off the restaurant balcony—landing right in the thick, humid rainforest below.

Samara's men leaned over the railing, firing wildly, but Maria and John had already vanished. Gabriel wasted no time. He took down the shooters, then shouted sharply, "Enough! Stop this now!"

The fire had finally settled, but everything was still so tangled. Gabriel and his mother had returned to his house, but their conversation quickly crossed every line.

"Gabriel, listen to me, please," Samara started. "How could she be alive? After all these years, she never once looked for you, which means she moved on without you. Well played!" Samara paused, then added, almost mocking, "To fake her own death like that. ……And me? I thought I was good at tricks but look at her."

"Quiet now," Gabriel shouted....

"Watch how you speak to me," Samara warned. "I'm still your mother!"

"Is that so? Really?" he said, then went on. "You know, Gloria wouldn't fake her death just like that. I don't know how she's alive or why she never came looking for me, but there's an explanation for everything. Right, Mom?" He looked at her seriously.

"What? Now I'm the target?" Samara shot back. Gabriel took a deep breath but couldn't hold back his anger. "I don't know," he said. "You tell me what you mean. What is it you want to say?" Just then, Lilly came in, and what she found didn't please her at all. "What's going on here, for God's sake? What's all this screaming?" she demanded.

"Now's not the time," Gabriel said, then stormed out of the house.

Lilly stood there, shock written all over her face. But for Samara, this was the moment she had been waiting for. She grabbed Lilly's hand firmly, her eyes focused. "We need to talk," she said, voice low and certain. "And trust me, after this, everything will be to your advantage." Lilly's lips curled into a sly smile—she always cared about one thing: how to turn any situation to benefit her.

Meanwhile, deep in the jungle, Maria and John were lost in a world that was as beautiful as it was unforgiving. The thick canopy above filtered the sunlight into shards of gold that danced across the vibrant green leaves. Strange birds called in the distance, their songs both haunting and enchanting. But danger lurked in every shadow. The air was humid, heavy with the scent of damp earth and blooming flowers.

Maria's breath came in shallow gasps, her body weak, crimson staining her clothes from the wound in her shoulder. John held her steady; his arm wrapped around her trembling form. He helped her rest on a fallen tree—its bark rough, covered in moss, and twisted with roots that seemed to have seen centuries pass. For a moment, silence fell, broken only by the distant rustle of unseen creatures moving through the undergrowth.

Maria's eyes met John's, tired but determined. Though her voice was barely a whisper, she tried to explain everything—each word heavy with urgency and pain.

"John, I —" …Maria started, but he cut her off. "Stop, stop, don't waste your strength. Everything will be fine, just try to hold on, please." As he helped her rest, John heard rustling in the bushes and footsteps running through the trees. "Who's there?" he called out, eyes scanning everywhere. With her last bit of strength, Maria spotted a little girl dressed strangely, standing near John—but before she could say a word, she lost consciousness.

"Hey, hey, hey! Stay with me!" John said, holding Maria, trying to bring her back. Then he heard a child's voice. "Calm down, she'll be fine," the girl said. John turned around, unsure how to react when he saw her. "I told you, calm down," the girl continued. "I'm here to take you to a safe place. But only if you trust me." With that, she turned and started walking. After a few steps, she stopped, looked back, and asked, "So, are you coming?" John was hesitant and confused but couldn't leave Maria like that. Needing help, he lifted her into his arms and followed the girl.

Back at Gabriel's house, the storm was far from over. "What?" Lilly said, glaring at Samara with contempt. "You heard me,"

Samara replied, then added, "The deal's good. Very good. With your help, I'll finish her—and then I vanish from your lives. You won't see me again."

"That might be the problem," Lilly snapped, then calmed down and went on, "If you hadn't come at all to visit us, none of this would be our problem. Our life here was perfect. Why would we get involved in your mess?"

Lilly didn't hold back. "Why don't you just leave right now and let us be? If she's out there in the forest, shot, there's no way she'll survive. So why don't you pack your things and get out of here? Now. Gabriel and I will go on with our lives, and you can deal with your problems—on your own." She pointed coldly toward the door. Samara said nothing, just stared back with a calm, unreadable look, and slapped her across the face.

"Stupid girl," Samara said....

Lilly couldn't believe it. "How dare you," she said, holding her cheek.

But before she could finish, Samara slapped her again, but on the other side of her face.

"Don't you even dare open your mouth," Samara's shouted. "You're so blind, it's almost pathetic. Maybe Gloria's my problem, but sweetheart, she's yours too. You really think you know Gabriel? Where do you imagine he is right now? Out for a casual stroll? No. Right now, Gabriel is lost—he doesn't even know where he is. But he's hunting. Desperate, relentless, searching every shadow, every corner, for her. And trust me, he will find her. No matter what."

Then she stepped closer and spoke again. "My son was weak when he first met her—too human, just like his father. He looks so much like him." She paused, for a moment, then added with a softened voice, almost bitter. "But that's exactly what you love about him, isn't it? Despite the dirty deals you both get into, despite your little betrayals, you know he's not like anyone else."

Lilly's shock was visible—how did Samara know so much? But Samara didn't stop.

"And as for Gabriel… Gloria—she means everything to him…. Even I'm not that important anymore, because she took that right away from me. What about you? Have you ever stopped to think what's left for you? So, either you help me finish this before Gabriel finds her, or I'll risk everything and do it myself. And you… you'll just stand there, drowning in regret, wishing you'd taken my deal."

After everything Samara said, Lilly took a long breath, her eyes drowned in sorrow. "Alright. You made a strong point. I'll take your deal. I'll make the calls — bring together a team who knows the jungle inside out. Tomorrow morning, we move."

Samara's gaze didn't soften. "Good. But don't underestimate Gloria. She's not just smart — she's dangerous."

Lilly smirked, and with a sarcastic tone added, "I'm always ready, mother. You don't have to worry about me. But maybe you should worry about what happens if Gabriel shows up while we're there."

Chapter 11

Maria and John stumbled into a secluded village, it felt as if the world had forgotten this place. The villages' tribe greeted them with a warmth that melted away their fatigue, and they gently guided Maria to a cozy hut to care for her. John found himself captivated by their simple, yet profoundly meaningful way of life. An elder, with a gentle smile, approached him and said: "So, you've lost your way, have you?"

"Not quite lost," John replied with a soft chuckle, "more like rescued from an awkward moment." The elder nodded knowingly and handed him a cup filled with a mysterious blend. "Drink this," she encouraged, her eyes twinkling, "it will soothe you and let your worries drift away, even if just for a moment."

John drank the mixture, but something strange happened. He thought they were speaking English the whole time—but in truth, he was speaking their language without even realising it.

"Who exactly are you?" he asked, watching the children run and laugh, completely carefree.

The old woman smiled softly. "We are simple people, living in harmony with nature. Deeply awakened. We understand the real meaning of life."

"What do you mean by that?" John asked, puzzled.

She looked him straight in the eyes—warm, gentle, but piercing.

"Have you ever asked yourself why you're here on this Earth?" she said, ringing with something deeper. "What your mission is? Your true purpose? You see… we're not born just to be ruled by the laws we made for ourselves. We're here for something far greater."

John listened closely, letting her words sink in. For the first time, he truly asked himself, "why am I here? What is my mission? What is my purpose?"

They were questions most people didn't even stop to consider anymore. Not in a world spinning so fast, where the rush of everyday life leaves no space for reflection. It was like his mind had slowed down just enough for him to finally hear that quiet voice inside. Night had fallen. John sat quietly, watching Maria as she slept, a part of him was still angry —frustrated by everything left unsaid, everything that didn't make sense. At the same time… he knew her well enough by now. Well enough to see the goodness in her. That deep, steady kind of good that doesn't just vanish, and whatever had happened—whatever truth was buried under the surface—he believed there had to be a reason.

On the other hand, Lilly was preparing carefully for the day ahead—but she wasn't the only one. Gabriel was making moves of his own. He had his own network, people he trusted—ruthless, experienced, and ready. As for Samara, she was alone in her room. One hand gripped a glass of whiskey. The other held an old photograph. She stared at it in silence as tears slid down her cheeks, uninvited. It was a photo of her and her husband, young and full of life—captured in a moment that felt like it belonged to a different couple.

"Taken from me," Samara whispered to herself, staring at the photo. "This cruel world took you—and your son—away from me."

At that moment, another voice broke the solace. "You know that's not true, ma'am."

"Antonio," Samara said quickly, wiping her tears away. "Since when do you forget your manners? You should knock before entering."

"Sorry, ma'am," he replied. "I did knock, but maybe you didn't hear me."

He stepped forward, standing right in front of her.

"Did you come here to judge me, Antonio?" she asked, her eyes sunken and black.

"Just because everyone's judging me right now… that's why you're here again, isn't it?" Samara added.

"I'm not here to judge you," Antonio said quietly. "But before tomorrow, I owe you the truth. Because I might not be alive to tell you after."

"What truth?" Samara asked, then added, "There is only one truth."

"Tomorrow, I won't let that Gloria win," she said firmly.

"But you won't gain anything from that victory," Antonio replied. "Gabriel will be twice as broken afterward—and you know that."

"I know, but I tried," she said, lowering her neck. Then she added, "I tried to make him strong, to prepare him for this cruel world. I thought I finally succeeded. Everything was going well… until the ghosts started to appear."

"How is she still alive? I can't understand that."

"I told you then, and I'm asking you now……Are you sure you want to go through with this tomorrow?" Antonio asked, testing her resolve.

"Antonio, of course I'm sure, but this time I'm the one who's going to finish things," she said confidently.

"Ma'am, sometimes we let hatred control us, and because of that, we forget to see the good around us—everything seems scary and dangerous," he replied.

"Oh, please," she interrupted. "I don't have pink-coloured glasses. I don't see it as all wonderful—I see it exactly as it is," she added.

"Ma'am, with all due respect, I've been by your side from the very beginning, even when Mr. Diego was alive. You weren't always this harsh…. I don't think you always see the world clearly. Sometimes, it's your fear that perceives for you. You know people are at the centre of it all—not the world, the people took your Diego from you, the people who made the wrong choices. And you know that."

"Stop! Don't, Antonio!" she said, looking at him seriously.

"Ma'am, as I said, with all due respect, I'm obliged to tell you the truth. I'm scared too," he continued. "That's why, all these years, I've stood by your side. We destroyed, sold, hurt—and all for what? Just so we wouldn't end up broken or wounded ourselves, by the very same people who think like us, who carry the same fears and doubts. It's a painful truth we live with every day... It may seem strange to you, but ma'am, Miss. Lilly is a copy of you. And you see it too. You might say she's young and naive, or maybe she just likes hurting people—but everything has its time. Nothing is forever, ma'am."

Antonio got ready to leave, but before he did, he asked, "Think carefully, ma'am. Are you willing to sacrifice your son again tomorrow?" With those words, he left Samara deep in thought.

The next morning, in the small village, John woke up and went straight to see Maria—but she wasn't there. At the hut, the little girl who had found them tugged his hand and said, pointing to the hills, "Is she the one you're looking for?" John looked at the girl, then glanced aside to see a hill with a temple where Maria and an old man were talking quietly, deeply focused.

She's talking with the teacher, the little girl told him, then added, "You'll see her later, but now come eat," teasing him as she gently pulled him along.

Samara and Lilly were already ready and set out for the hunt. Gabriel was ready too, well prepared, as he also headed into the jungle, but his orders were strict: "Don't let anyone stand in your way," Gabriel told them. One of his close friends asked, "But brother, what if your mother is there, or someone close shows up?" Gabriel answered with a finality, "I said no one," and then they moved out.

At that time, Maria asked the Old Man, "Where exactly are we, and why are you glowing like that?" The Old Man smiled and said, "I'm not glowing. You're just seeing my aura." Then he added, "That's a good thing. Not everyone can see it. Usually, only children can, because they are pure beings."

Maria blushed for a moment and looked down. "I'm not so pure. I tried to start over, but my past wouldn't let me," she said.

"It's not a mistake to start over, dear child. Sometimes life puts us in situations we don't want to be in. But life always sends you things exactly when you're not ready—just to see if you'll manage and if you'll keep that innocent childlike flame inside you after every challenge. The flame everyone has when they come to this planet Earth… or another space," he said.

"What do you mean?" she asked.

"I mean that you know this planet is just one of many in the multiverse, and that our souls are much more than just bodies. The body dies, but the soul doesn't," he said.

"I don't understand," she said, uncertain.

"I think you do, Gloria," he replied calmly.

Her name floated in the silence between them, familiar yet strange. She couldn't believe she was hearing it again.

"But… how?" she asked, searching his eyes for an answer she couldn't quite grasp.

He looked at her gently, steady and kind.

"How do I know? I know everything. But you already know that... After all you've been through, holding onto that small flame inside—you've done something few can. Because it's easy to let anger, fear, and bitterness swallow you whole. To shut down and become distant, cold, like a machine built only to survive. That's the world we live in. Not just here, Gloria. It's the same everywhere you go. Our souls come here pure, overflowing with love—for everything and everyone. But life changes us. As we grow, we learn to hide behind masks. Some are placed on us by parents, others by teachers, and many by friends. Masks we wear just to belong, just to be accepted somewhere." he said.

She looked at him deeply and said, "That's wrong, because we have to accept ourselves first. When we do, there's no more waiting or changing masks just to be accepted. We'll feel at peace everywhere—because we truly know ourselves."

"Exactly," he replied, "but it's not easy." He went on, "It takes a lot of courage, because people often know more about others than about themselves. We know what others like, what they hate, and so on—which isn't bad—but first, we have to truly know ourselves too......That's where many fail.......To really know yourself, to be honest no matter the situation, to stay loyal and not blinded by material things—that's a hard path for many."

"I understand," she said, looking away as she spotted John in the distance.

"Go," the Elder said, "go and explain to him. He will understand," he added.

Maria paused as she stood and started to walk, but the Elder spoke again.

"Oh, and my dear child, don't be afraid of the coming battle."

"What?" she whispered, confused.

"Everything will fall into place, but after that, you'll face a difficult choice," the Elder added.

As Maria turned to face him, he was gone.

"Strange," she thought. "Where did he disappear too so quickly?"

Chapter 12

*M*eanwhile, in the jungle, Lilly's people had already found traces—but did they know that Gabriel's people were following right behind?

Maria approached John, her heart pounding with courage and hope.

"Hey... can we talk?" she whispered.

John turned slowly, his eyes searching hers. Without a word, he pulled her into a fierce hug, afraid to let go.

"I was so scared... I thought I lost you," he said, his voice shaking.

She held him just as tightly, letting the moment last. After a while, they moved to sit on the hill near the temple.

"I'm sorry I never told you... not from the start," Maria began.

"How could this be possible? Did my uncle know?" John asked, still trying to understand.

"Yes," she nodded, "He was the one who helped me find myself again after everything. That secret room in your apartment… it's secret because I was the secret."

She paused, a faint, bittersweet smile crossing her lips.

"I even remember you, just a little—from when we were kids, playing cops and robbers."

"Yeah, strange, isn't it?" John said.

"Who would have thought life would pull us into a real game— and after all this time," he added.

"As they say, everything falls into place at the right time in the right moment," she replied.

"But where was I?" she continued, a faint smile touching her lips.

"Oh, right. After that, I became an archaeologist. A good one…. I was very close to your uncle—he was like a father to me…... One day, he found a man trying to escape from some bad people— gangsters or maybe mafia, we didn't really know. Your uncle, my grandmother, and I helped him because we thought those people wanted to finish him off…. Gabriel was a good soul. It didn't take long for us to fall for each other, but then we realised the people chasing him didn't want to kill or hurt him."

John looked at her with a sad face, already knowing he had feelings for her but unable to show them right then. Still, he didn't feel hate—just relief that she was safe.

"We found out those people didn't want to hurt Gabriel—they wanted him back." Maria continued …" Your uncle knew Samara well. She was one of those powerful figures who got whatever she wanted, but no one ever had proof. When we learned Gabriel was her son, it felt like the world shifted. And I… I fell even deeper for him, because he refused to become what she wanted. He stood his ground. But now I understand how far Samara was willing to go to bend him to her will…. That night, before I went home, Gabriel sent me a message—he was waiting at our spot. When I got there, I saw him get into his car, and then… the car exploded. My heart shattered. I couldn't breathe. I don't even remember how I got home…. My grandmother noticed right away. We went outside to catch some air, and I couldn't stop crying while she held me. Then, for a moment, she went back inside to grab a coat to wrap around me. And at that very moment, the house blew up…. I don't remember anything after that night. When I woke up, I was in a hospital, and your uncle was there beside me. No one except Lee knew I was alive. So, we decided to keep it that way, at least until we figured out who was behind it all. After we exposed and helped put behind bars some of the biggest mob bosses, including Samara, I thought my past was finally done with me. I left everything behind and started fresh in Manchester, living a quiet, simple life. Just trying to heal and find peace in the small moments, far away from everything……Then one day, I found an elderly woman on the street—robbed, broken, left like she didn't matter. I couldn't ignore her. For weeks, I cared for her with nothing expected in return. She was a fragile light in a dark world, a reminder that kindness still mattered… Later, I received a letter from her. She had passed, but in that letter, she left me everything she owned—a fortune beyond what I ever imagined. Not because of who I was, but because of those few weeks when I showed her real compassion. That inheritance made me a millionaire overnight, but more than money, it gave me a chance to rewrite my life. That's how I became Maria Cafero—carrying both the pain of my past and the hope of a new future, shaped by truth and kindness."

A quiet pause hung between them, the soft rustle of leaves around the old temple hills the only sound. She looked up at him, about to speak, "I'm sorry that…" but John's hand gently covered hers, stopping the words before they escaped. "Shhh… you don't have to say anything," he said quietly. His arms wrapped around her, warm and steady, and she let herself fall into the comfort of that embrace, the pressure of years and secrets being released, held safe between them.

"You didn't do anything wrong, Maria—or Gloria, no matter what name you carry. What matters is you're here, you're real." His voice was gentle, almost breaking. "You didn't know he was alive, and he didn't know you were either."

She met his eyes, pain and truth shining there. She stepped back just a little, resting her hands lightly on his chest, voice trembling. "I never meant to lie to you."

He brushed a stray curl from her face, eyes full of something fierce and tender all at once. "I know. But now… now we have to be ready. Because from this moment on, no one will let you slip away. Everyone knows you're alive. And they will come."

The wind whispered through the trees, the fading light casting long shadows around them—two souls caught in the quiet before the storm, bound by truth, fear, and a fragile hope that maybe, somehow, they could face whatever was coming together.

She lowered her head, then turned around—and the temple was gone. Only some crumbling walls remained, wrapped in thick vines. "What?" she whispered. John turned too, his eyes wide with disbelief at the strange sight. They both started scanning the jungle around them, searching. Maria studied the walls closely, her archaeologist's heart racing. "This can't be," she murmured to herself.

"Maria!" John called her over. She walked to his side. "The village is gone," he said quietly. They both stared into the dense jungle where nothing, but wild greenery stood—no sign of the village.

"But how? How is this even possible?" John asked, clearly shaken. "Just minutes ago, It was right here," he added, confused.

"If I'm not mistaken," Maria said, moving back to the walls, her voice cracking with excitement. John followed her, sensing the shift in her energy.

"I'm sure I'm right, John. These walls, these carvings—they're over five thousand years old."

"Five thousand? How…?" he asked, stunned.

"And if I'm right," she continued, "we're stuck in a time loop."

John looked around, still trying to grasp what they were seeing. Then he spoke softly, remembering a lesson from long ago. "My uncle once told me that time isn't just a line—past, present, and future all happen at once, layered on top of each other. Sometimes, places like this create a kind of… overlap, where moments from different times mix together. That's why it feels like we lost time. It's not really lost—it's caught in this loop, this time-lapse. We're standing in a place where time bends, where what was, what is, and what will be all exist right now."

John whispered to Maria, warning her after hearing the sound of cars. "We're not alone." She listened closely too, catching voices and the noise of engines roaring. "Your gun—do you have it?" he asked. "Yes, and yours?" she replied. "Yeah, come, let's hide." They moved toward the trees to take cover, but they weren't alone anymore—people were behind them.

So, as they hid in the jungle, the air heavy with humidity and the smell of wet earth, shapes danced between the dense trees. The tension, electric. John's ears picked up the faint sound of voices mixed with rustling leaves and snapping branches. Then he hears it—someone calling out, "Gloria!" His heart skips, as he turns to Maria, whispering urgently, "Maria, that's Gabriel." Around them, the jungle feels alive—birds scatter, insects buzz wildly, and the distant sounds of footsteps grow louder. Suddenly, from the underbrush, Lilly's men emerge, deadly and determined. The two groups collide violently; the crack of gunfire shatters the sticky air as bullets ricochet off trees and spray leaves like rain. Maria and John duck behind fallen trunks, feeling the sting of dirt and leaves kicked up by close shots. Mayhem erupts as Gabriel's men and Lilly's crew turn on each other, shouting, shooting, and crashing through vines and branches. The jungle is a battlefield—each step unknown, each sound their possible last. John's breath quickens as he strains to make out more voices. Then Maria hears it—a sharp command, "Hold her!"—Lilly's voice cutting through the chaos. The struggle closing in fast, with every second counting.

After some time of running and gunfire, Maria and John stumbled onto a high hill, surrounded on all sides with no escape. Below, a wide river roared, cutting off any chance to go further. From the left, Samara stepped forward, weapon steady, eyes cold and assessing. On the right, Lilly appeared, flanked by armed men, guns raised and ready. Then in front of them, Gabriel and his crew emerged, quickly silencing Lilly's men with swift shots. Lilly's laugh cut through the tension, defying and mocking. "So, you think you have your own army? Oh, Gabriel…" But the shock hit hard—Gabriel's men turned their guns on him, revealing they'd been Lilly's all along. The climate charged with betrayal, guns aimed and fingers tightening on triggers, Maria and John were caught right in the deadly middle.

"Well played," said Samara.

"Told you, Mommy, I'd take care of everything," Lilly replied.

"Get back!" shouted John, stepping in front of Maria to shield her.

"Stop!" Gabriel yelled from the other side.

At that moment, Samara truly saw herself in Lilly, the hatred, the pain and the emptiness in her eyes. What she saw—she didn't like at all…. she remembered Antonio's words "Are you willing to sacrifice your son again tomorrow?" with that she snapped, with a few quick shots, she took down Lilly's men. Gabriel was no longer targeted, the gun clicked empty. Samara dropped it to the ground beneath the trees and stepped forward.

Seeing this, Lilly angrily aimed her weapon at Samara.

"What do you think you're doing?" Lilly said.

"Something I won't regret," Samara replied.

"Lilly, don't!" Gabriel shouted.

"Me?" Lilly looked at him seriously. "So, you care more about her than about me!" Lilly said, upset.

In a flash, Lilly tried to shoot Gabriel, but Samara stepped in front of him—and the bullet struck Samara instead. John immediately took a defensive position and shot Lilly in the shoulder… She fell to the ground as well. Gabriel rushed to his mother, grabbed his gun, and aimed it at Lilly.

"Hey, Gabriel, stop!" Maria shouted, throwing down her gun and trying to intervene.

Lilly, though wounded, looked at Gabriel with a smirk.

"What's the matter?" she said, coughing lightly.

"Come on, shoot me!…... What are you waiting for?" she taunted him.

Just as no one expected it, Gabriel delivered his final blow—and killed her.

Maria couldn't believe it. The shock hit her like a wave she didn't have time to brace for. John immediately turned his gun on Gabriel and shielded Maria behind him. But before anyone could react, more of Samara's people appeared from the jungle. In a flash, they shot Gabriel—they didn't even know who they were aiming at. John tried to defend himself, but there were too many. He and Maria jumped straight off the hill and landed in the rushing river. Antonio arrived, but what he saw shocked him so deeply it felt like a knife stabbing his heart. The people he loved most were already dead.

Maria and John were drifting with the river's current—Maria at one end, John at the other. Then John called out to Maria with all his strength, trying not to lose sight of her.

"John!" she shouted back loudly, doing her best not to lose sight of him either.

Then they noticed the same little girl running along the riverbank again.

Down by the river, the people from the village- the same village that later disappeared—were waiting. Together, they pulled Maria and John out of the water. Neither of them could believe what had happened.

They returned to the village, both exhausted.

Chapter 13

As evening came, the same old woman who had spoken to John before entered their hut where Maria and John were staying. She offered them drinks to help calm their nerves, but they refused. The old woman left and went to the temple to meet the teacher.

Meditating, the teacher sensed the old woman's presence behind him.

"How are they?" he asked.

"Teacher ……are you sure they will be ready and agree to this?" the old woman asked him.

"Yes," he said calmly, adding, "I'm sure. In a battle like this, we need not just warriors, but warriors with hearts. Let them rest tonight. They've been through a lot today. Tomorrow is a new day, and every new day brings a new beginning. Morning is always wiser than evening."

"All right, teacher," the old woman said, and she left.

And so, everything went on. That day burned a lot of pain into many people, but still, everyone was prepared for some kind of end. After all, every beginning and every end depends solely on our own decisions, which aren't always easy, but we must always be responsible and honest with ourselves. Because only when we are honest with ourselves, we free ourselves from all the fears we hide that keep us in the dark. Only when we truly know and accept ourselves— and are ready for change, as change is such a big part of growing for the better—do we understand that we don't need masks just to be accepted by the world. Life goes on without us. Work goes on without us. Wealth, property, and fame go on and were here before us and will remain after us. So how we choose to live our lives and what we dedicate ourselves to—whether work, relationships, fame, or wealth—or simply finding balance and enjoying all these things without losing ourselves, that depends only on us.

At dawn, with the first rays of the sun, Maria and John stood before the temple, and in front of them stood the teacher. "Do you know where you are?" he asked.

"We think so," Maria began, and John added, "But how is this even possible?"

The teacher smiled gently and replied, "Everything is possible." With that, he stepped aside as a man they never expected to see appeared before them.

"Lee?" Maria said in surprise. "Uncle?" John whispered.

"Yes, it's me." He said, the two rushed to embrace him, then stepped back.

"But how?" Maria asked. "I don't understand. I was the one who buried you," John said.

"There is an explanation for everything," Lee said with a smile.

"But now, there are more important things we need to discuss." he added.

Maria and John exchanged glances, with no idea what was coming next....

To be continued.......

Every new day is a chance to begin again. None of us are perfect—that's the beauty of being human. We stumble, we fall, but through our mistakes, we learn what truly matters. Too often, fear, pride, anger, and envy take hold, pulling our strings. But the truth is, we hold the power. We are the ones who must take back control. Don't let your inner child's key lie forgotten or fall into the wrong hands. Deep inside, you know why you're here. You were born with a purpose, even if you've forgotten it along the way.

So, wake up. Look within. Shake your soul until the answers rise. It's not easy—change never is. But change is also a gift—it's what gives you the strength to break free, to grow beyond who you were, and to finally find yourself. Don't let your life slip away hidden behind the masks you wear to please the world. Have the courage to take them off. To stand raw and real. And with each sunrise, discover a little more of who you truly are. Because in the end, the only mask worth wearing is the one you choose to leave behind.

This book is for those who hear a quiet call within—a call to awaken, to look beyond the surface, and to meet the deeper self that many of us hide from. It's for the brave souls who sense that something needs to change but struggle to accept that truth inside. I wrote this story for anyone who's ever felt lost, confused, or afraid to face their own shadows.

Through these pages, I hope you've found a mirror—a way to see yourself with compassion and courage. Because awakening isn't just about knowing who you are; it's about having the strength to change, to break free from the masks that bind you, and to step into your true self. Change is the gift that gives you power—not to become someone new, but to finally become who you were always meant to be.

If you've journeyed with me until the end, maybe you're ready to stop running and start living fully—without fear, without disguise. The path won't always be easy, but it will be real, honest, and deeply yours. This is your invitation to begin again, to find your own light, and to embrace the beautiful, messy truth of YOU……

www.ingramcontent.com/pod-product-compliance
Lightning Source LLC
Chambersburg PA
CBHW031156010826
48971CB00012B/745